CONVERGING LINES

Geoff Tarrant

The second novel in the History Detective series.

'Just one person to thank. She pushed when pushing was needed, gave me space when it was required and managed to edit the whole thing with patience and humour. So - grazie mille Alanna. A thousand thanks. '

Prelude

My name is Joseph Fourier but this is not my story. I am a mathematician by calling and I have lived a long and prosperous life largely in the service of the Emperor Napoleon. In order to understand more clearly what I am about to relate it is necessary to give you a little of my background. I was born in Auxerre in 1768 to a poor family but became an orphan at the age of 9. At the start of the Revolution some twenty years later I was active initially in my own district serving on the local Revolutionary Council. I later moved to Paris but then during the Reign of Terror, I was imprisoned when I argued against the new policy of mass arrests and executions. It was really quite ironic. The Council at the time was made up of two factions who were struggling with each other for control. The leader of the controlling group was a man called Maximilien Robespierre and I managed to obtain an audience with him to argue my case. Even if I say so myself, I argued passionately and eloquently for my life to be spared but to no avail. I was sent back to my cell to wait for the trek to the guillotine. As things transpired it was only a matter of days later that control was wrested from the faction in charge and Robespierre himself was executed. This however, is not his story either. It is, in fact, the story of a man who was appointed by Robespierre to prosecute me. His name is Antoine Lestrade.

1

The wind had been blowing from the south since early afternoon. It was a wind that rattled the windows and found the gaps even though I had only recently moved in to my newly built home. I was wealthy enough to be able to afford the luxuries that were on offer to a man of my station but not so much so that I drew the unwanted attention of the Committee. The candles spluttered but stayed alight as I waited for that knock on the door. At this time of night, for most citizens, it would be a moment of horror - a portention of their impending bloody death. In this case though, the visitor was expected albeit his arrival would signal the start of a new phase in my life. The year was 1794 and this was the town of Versailles just 20 kilometres from Paris and 'La Terreur' - the so called 'Reign of Terror' was at its height.
 Anyone who came to the attention of the Committee of Public Safety would likely be facing an appointment with 'Madame Guillotine'. Already, tens of thousands had met an untimely end - often for the most trivial of reasons. Earlier

that day I had heard that my mentor Maximilien Robespierre, one of the most powerful and respected members of the Committee, had been executed after losing an internal struggle for control.

My name is Antoine Lestrade and like Robespierre, I was a practising lawyer. We had met a number of years before and had become firm friends, both determined to represent a class of people who could little afford legal representation. At first it had been a difficult and arduous struggle, not made any easier by Robespierre's political ambitions but then, just five years ago he had been elected to serve in the National Constituent Assembly. At the time it was a toothless body, laughed at and disparaged by the ruling classes - those toads who surrounded the King and his Queen - Marie Antoinette.

The council could make as many declarations and proclamations as it wished but they were ignored and ridiculed. Then, my friend Maximilien was elected as President of the so called Jacobin Club which became famous as the breeding ground of the revolution and his attacks on the Monarchy and his insistence on reform became more and more popular.

As rapid as his rise to power had been, the fall of Robespierre had been shocking in it's precipitancy. I had last spoken to him one week ago and although the struggle in the Committee between extremist factions was coming to a head, there had been no indication of the bloody events that were to occur. The details were unclear but the story that I had heard from a friend who had raced out from Paris to warn me, told of a coup that had forced Robespierre and his supporters into the Hotel de Ville, pursued by troops sent by the elements of the Revolutionary Council who were opposing them. As the soldiers entered the government

3

building, Robespierre had tried to escape from a window only to fall breaking both of his legs. In agony he had been dragged back inside, continuing to shout defiance. A musket had been fired at him and the ball had smashed the lower part of his cheekbone. A doctor had been summoned and his face had been wrapped in bandages to stem the bleeding. He had spent the night in a semi-conscious stupor but the morning after he had been made to face his accusers. It little mattered that he was unable to speak in order to defend himself, the council had already made the decision - Robespierre was to be executed that very day. It was said that in order to clear the way for the guillotine blade to fall upon his neck, the executioner had ripped the facial bandage away causing the most heart rending scream of anguish which was instantly silenced as the blade fell.

It was clear to me that anyone who had been associated with Robespierre would be rounded up in the ensuing cull and would face a demise that was just as bloody. I was determined that this was not to be my fate. It was little known I hoped but there were also a host of other reasons that I could be indicted by the Committee. My past history was chequered to say the least and I had been forced to forage favours wherever I could find them.

I looked at the clock again. It was an expensive luxury but one that I felt gave a certain pre-eminence to my home. Sadly, today's events confirmed that it would be a long time after this night before I would be able return here again. I had been expecting this day to arrive for some time. If it hadn't been the fall of Robespierre, there could have been any one of a myriad of reasons in these troubled times that would have forced me to flee for my life. I had prepared as well as I had been able. There was a trunk containing part of my

4

wealth and belongings waiting for me at the port of Rouen. Letters had been written and documents signed that would ensure that my sister, who together with her husband also resided here, would take over proprietorship of the house. In fact the only reason that I was still here and not riding west was because of the impending arrival of my expected visitor.

I lifted my head as I thought I heard a sound. It was too early for my visitor who was always punctilious with his timekeeping. At first I thought that I had been mistaken but there it was again. Raised voices in the distance - carried and distorted by the wind. It was not a good sign. At this time of night it was rare to hear even the watchmen conversing in low tones. Then, taps on the door. Two quick raps, a pause followed by a third. The signal had been agreed many days earlier and so with some misgiving I rose from my chair and unlatched the door.

'Quickly - let me inside then extinguish the candles.'

The man who had spoken was roughly dressed, an incongruity when compared with his smooth mellifluous voice. I knew him by his surname of Guillot, a man who had been cast down by the aristocracy many years before but who had taken his revenge by thievery. Only the choicest, most rare and valuable artefacts had been his target over the years and particularly, only those owned by the people who he felt had contributed towards his abandonment from the society which had raised him. He had been befriended by me under the most strange set of circumstances and I in turn had admired this man who had chosen to extract some of the immense wealth from the buffoons who chose to party and socialise while most of France starved.

* * *

Guillot was not a remarkable man to look at - medium height - medium build and a bland face with no characterising features. In other words instantly forgettable, which of course was an immense asset in his line of work. His problem came when he started to speak, when it was obvious to even the most extreme dunderhead that his background was much more refined than his appearance had led them to believe. Far enough away from the Capital this was not a handicap as the assumption from the scarcely travelled population was that this was a normal Parisian merchants accent. It was only in his home city that it became problematic and then he had been forced to adopt the guise of a mute. The problem of course was that not being able to speak had presented more difficulties than it had solved and so he had been required to adopt the harsh, guttural voice of the downtrodden Parisian citizen. At first, people had questioned this strange tone but over time it had become more relaxed and natural. Now, he was able to switch between the two at will.

It was obvious as he entered that all was not well. Normally a relaxed and cheerful character, this time his voice was strained and his face was troubled. The candles smoked as they were extinguished.

'What is the problem?' I asked.

No formalities were needed between us - we had known each other for many years and the climate of revenge and death that was prevalent at the moment meant conventional form and niceties were superfluous.

'At first, all went well. They had left only three soldiers to guard the Petit Trianon, the home of Madame Deficit.'

'Even though she has been executed, I do wish you would

refer to the Queen by her proper name.' Even in the dark, the irritation that crept across my face was obvious.

'Pah! That bitch has a thousand names amongst the people that I deal with that are much worse than that.'

It was true that the late Queen was blamed for many of France's troubles but strangely, she was hated only by a minority and still loved by many. Guillot definitely fell into the former category but I was one of the latter. Our friendship had remained despite this fundamental difference between us.

'So what went wrong?'

'As I expected, the soldiers had lit a fire and were drinking and playing cards when I crept by. I worked my way around to the rear of the mansion and entered the rooms that she had used as her apartment. Amazingly, they were untouched - a fact that despite the threat of an agonising death to anyone who entered them, I find astonishing. Even I was unnerved at first. Every time I turned around, I faintly saw a figure - my reflection in the numerous mirrors that decorated the place. I collected what I could carry and made my way back out. It was at this point that I was discovered. This blasted wind had whipped the clouds across, uncovering the moon, making the grounds as bright as daylight. One of the soldiers had a mastiff at his feet and the dog saw my movement between the trees. I was forced to flee with a hue and cry behind me and I was followed into the town. I managed to evade them but they are now carrying out a house to house search and it will only be a matter of time before they arrive here.'

* * *

I paused for several seconds in order to gather my thoughts before answering.

'No matter. It just means that we need to bring our plans forward. We must ride quickly out of town. Are you still planning to head south?'

'Yes. I have property in Bordeaux where my connections to Paris are unknown. If I wish to do so, I have accumulated enough wealth to settle down quietly.'

Despite the circumstances I couldn't help but smile to myself. The thought of Guillot settling down anywhere was ridiculous. I was convinced that his 'revenge on the aristocracy' was simply a justification for a life that he would have chosen anyway. Guillot had found his calling. For some people it was the Law, for others the Church. This man thrived on the adventure and danger that were a consequence of a life of crime. The incidental fact that his victims were the richest in the land simply helped to ease his conscience and to line his pockets more quickly.

'And you are still determined to head for the Colonies?'

I considered for a moment before replying.
    'This country is too dangerous for me now. My associations with both the late Queen and with Robespierre mean that every dog in the Committee will want my head on a pikestaff. The only reason that I have been safe so far was because of the protection of my mentor. How things swing so quickly. I will leave and return at some point in the future when events, as they must, will have settled down. Everything is prepared - I just have to get to Rouen. Now, have you got the Bohmer and Bassange necklace for me? It is

all that I want - the rest of the spoils are yours.'

Guillot passed me a bag made of blue velvet and closed with a drawcord. A quick glance revealed to me that it contained the piece of jewellery that was at the heart of the scandal that had occurred 18 years earlier. A scandal into which I had been drawn and had almost not escaped. The necklace was beautiful and it was said that the largest collection of diamonds ever accumulated in one place had been needed to construct it. I knew it well and immediately pulled the string closed.

I thought for a moment then spoke. 'Go and get the horses ready. I have one or two things to do then I will join you.' Guillot stood and walked to the back door that led to the stables.

'Be quick then. They will be here shortly.'

In the few minutes since the arrival of my friend, I had come to a decision. I was not at all sure that capture wasn't inevitable. I still hoped that my dealings with Queen Marie Antoinette might only be known to a few and there was an outside chance that my friendship with Robespierre might be overlooked. If I were caught however, I would not be able to explain the necklace that I would have in my possession and it would certainly guarantee my trip to the guillotine. I listened for a moment. The voices in the distance had grown louder and were not far away now. I strode to the staircase and entered my chambers above. I was a cautious man and since acquiring the house I had created a secure space in a wall cavity in which I was able to hide my most valuable possessions. Unless you were aware of its presence it was invisible and secure. I moved to its location and pushed and twisted. The block moved to one side revealing a space that was a handspan from top to bottom. It was empty. All of its contents waited for me in Rouen. Pausing for a moment I placed the velvet bag inside and repeated the complex twisting and pulling motion that was required to restore the wall to its previous state. There was no time to speak to my sister. When the soldiers arrived it would be better if she and her husband looked as if they had been disturbed from their sleep. They would also have the sense to give my location as Paris - a not infrequent occurrence these days.

With one last look around the room I retraced my steps downstairs. I pulled on my riding boots and a cape and walked to the door which had been opened by Guillot a few minutes earlier. Across the yard he was waiting, standing beside two saddled horses. We exchanged a glance and mounted. The voices were very close now - odd words and phrases could be made out and it was obvious that the thief was the object of their ire. The soldiers that had been on guard at the Queen's palace would be severely reprimanded if it were proved that they had been derelict in their duty. The town of Versailles was not large, mainly just a collection of buildings that had grown up around the grand Palace of Versailles. The construction of the Palace had required masons and labourers, its grounds a vast army of gardeners and food and materials needed to be brought in from Paris. At first the buildings were just a ramshackle, motley collection but over time more wealthy families had built their residences there and like mine there were now a number of more stately, stone built homes. It did make escape more difficult though. The tread of the horses was muffled by the mud, and the wind carried any sound that they made away from the search parties. The clouds though, were treacherous, providing dark shadows for cover one moment but then revealing the full moon which flooded the area the next. We had to work our way towards the eastern edge before we were seen for the first time.

A shout of 'arretez' was clearly heard and the dogs that accompanied their pursuers began to bay. It would be a few more minutes before we would clear all of the buildings and be able to hide ourselves in the surrounding forest but at that moment it was unclear which was the safest direction in which to head. I made the decision when I saw a group of people ahead, between us and the safety of the woodland. I swung my horse back towards the palace and growled. 'Follow me.'

We abandoned the stealth with which we had started and urged our horses to pick up speed. Swerving right then left around the wooden houses we headed towards the south. Shouts could now be heard all around us and it was unclear which was the safest route to take. If we could only get out of town I thought, we would be clear. No one knew who it was that they were pursuing - our identities were unknown. A group ahead and the sound of a musket being discharged startled us and we swung our horses left again putting more buildings behind us. The perimeter was now getting closer and we could see the woodland beyond the last remaining houses. We pushed our horses into a gallop and rode for safety. More shots rang out as we burst into the open with the safety of the forest just a hundred metres away. It was as we were entering the canopy of the first trees that Guillot's horse fell, hit by a musket ball. I pulled my own horse to a halt, galloped back and was about to hoist Guillot on to the back of my mount when I saw the bloodstain on his clothing. He also had been hit and lay still on the ground alongside the dying animal.

Converging Lines

2

There was no time for thought. A crowd of people had emerged from behind the ramshackle houses and were running in our direction. To add to the confusion and chaos, those soldiers with pistols that had not yet been discharged were pointing them at us. The supine body on the ground gave credence to the rumour that the accuracy of these devices had improved somewhat over the last year or two. There was a crack and then another and balls of lead could be heard thumping into the trees nearby.

I crouched down, scooping my arms underneath the inert body. I lifted and threw my companion across the front of the saddle of my own horse. For all I knew, Guillot could be dead but that could be ascertained later. The friendship between us meant that I was unable to leave the thief to his fate. Another crack and this time I heard the whistle of the lead ball as it passed over my head. Another crack and splinters of wood from a nearby branch flew by. With no thought other than to get away I thrust my boot into the stirrup, swung onto what little of the saddle remained available and urged my horse to ride between the trees, swinging this way and that to put as much woodland between us and the pursuers as possible.

After ten minutes riding in a westerly direction we emerged onto a track that was leading away from the town and in the direction of the port. I swung the horse to follow this easier route. By this time the clouds had filled the sky and the strong wind was driving a freezing rain across their path. I daren't stop yet to check on Guillot's condition - there was no telling whether the pursuers might try this route. There were only a limited number of trails through the forest that a horse could comfortably follow. It was my hope that the excitement over the capture of what were thought to be petty thieves would die away and everyone would return to their beds where it would be much warmer than it was out here. Nonetheless, I couldn't risk stopping yet and so I rode as best I could whilst holding onto the body in front of me, trying to stop it slipping down onto the ground. It was not an easy task and made progress particularly slow. We were slowed down further each time we came to a hamlet with just a smattering of houses. Although I expected no harm from the woodcutters and charcoal burners, I did not want our direction to be discovered in case pursuit was continued in the morning. As a result I considered it to be judicious to circumnavigate these clearings and this also took time.

As I was not expected at the port for another two days the extra hours were not going to cost me. At last, coming across a ruined cottage by the side of the road, I decided that enough time and distance had elapsed that I could consider the condition of poor Guillot. I pulled up the horse, carefully dismounted, fastening the reigns of the animal to a branch. It would be a disaster to lose the mount at this stage. Guillot slid easily into my arms and I lowered the body to the ground. Trained as a lawyer my medical knowledge was practically nil but I was able to ascertain two things. First of all Guillot was still alive. The faint, rasping breathing told me that. It also told me however, that all was not well. Further probing showed that the lead ball had scoured the man's side before entering the upper arm. A lot of blood had been lost and the wounds continued to bleed slowly. However, there was nothing else for it. The journey had to be completed and perhaps a surgeon could be found in Rouen.

The rest of the journey was slow and arduous and by the time that the first calling of the birds had started to indicate the arrival of dawn, I was cold, wet and thoroughly miserable. The winds that had scudded the clouds around yesterday evening had developed into a strong steady roar making progress even more uncomfortable. I stopped twice again to check on the condition of my companion but found little change. By now the occurrence of the hamlets had become more frequent and I decided to simply ride through them hoping that Rouen would not be too far away. Once in the port I hoped that I could relax a little and find medical help for Guillot. It was late morning before the woodland gave way to cultivated fields and the walls of Rouen could be seen in the distance. The misery caused by the wet and cold had given way to an ache in my stomach, indicating that a long time had passed since my last meal. A decision had to made. The ship that I was bound for was not due to leave until the following day and I had planned to arrive at the last minute. With this change in circumstances I now decided to make directly for the quayside and hope that the surgeon and Captain were both on board. The gates to the town were open and unguarded as we rode through. The route down to the river passed by houses that indicated a prosperous populace but as we emerged onto the quayside the quietness of the morning gave way to a hustle and bustle as ships were being prepared for embarkation on the morning tide. I had last seen the clipper that was to depart for the American Colonies just a week earlier when I had paid for my passage with gold. My belongings had been left in the home of a distant relative within the town with arrangements being made for their delivery to the ship just hours before it's departure. The clipper was on the far side of the quay, swaying in the wind, it's bare masts and rigging looking like a picture of the bones of a whale that I had once seen.

Men who were scurrying back and forth carrying bundles of this and barrels of that scarcely glanced at the figure lying across the front of the horse. In these times it was dangerous to ask too many questions and so people preferred to simply go about their own business.

It was only a matter of minutes before I was able to dismount again. This time I handed the horse's reins and a small coin to a boy, who was stood watching the tall ship, with instructions that if all was well when I returned there would be more to follow. After riding for many hours through the inclement conditions I took less care with Guillot, simply slinging him across one shoulder and with one arm around his legs walked towards the vessel. As I mounted the gangplank, which was no easy task with a deadweight about your shoulders, the ship's boatswain appeared above me. Fortunately the man had been present when I had met with the Captain the week previously and recognised me immediately.

* * *

'Monsieur Lestrade. It looks as though you have trouble on your hands.'

'More likely in them.' I growled in return. 'Are the Captain and more importantly, the surgeon aboard?'

'Captain Jones is with the port authority at the moment but should be back shortly. The surgeon is in his cabin - sober or otherwise.'

'Sober I hope. I have work for him. Can you take me to him?'

The boatswain turned in the direction of the companionway which led from the lower to the upper deck and stepping over ropes and around barrels that were yet to be stowed away we soon reached the cabin of the man who would decide the ultimate fate of Guillot. Many musket wounds were fatal, not because of the damage that they caused to bone and tissue but because of infections that set in afterwards. If the surgeon so decreed it, then Guillot would simply be left to fester away.

When the boatswain tapped on the door I was relieved to hear the steady voice of a man who did not appear to have succumbed to the boredom of waiting for departure and as we entered the confined space I took in a figure who was sat at a rustic desk, reading a somewhat weighty tome.

'Hmm. It looks as though you have work for me. Tell me what has happened'.

He only listened for a few moments before stopping my explanation saying, 'I don't want to know the details - bring him along here to the surgery where I see my patients. Luckily for him, I am a trained doctor and not just a sawmaster so please don't refer to me as the surgeon. And if this idiot made any reference to me not being sober ignore him completely. The humour is tired and poor. I have to deal with the effects of alcohol on this crew too many times for me to enjoy it myself.'

I did as I was bidden and when I lay Guillot out on a wooden trestle I was told that Doctor Shaw, for that was his name, would do the best that he could then report back when there was any news.

By this time the boatswain had disappeared and I was left to find my own way out onto the main deck. The narrow corridors and confined spaces that I glimpsed did little to put me at ease. Fleeing to the American Colonies was not a decision that I had made lightly but my knowledge of sailing vessels matched my knowledge of medicine and I couldn't see how a ship like this could survive a journey that could take several weeks in rough seas. The die was cast however and I was certain that my life expectancy, if I remained in France, would be limited. It was time for a change. A new life in the Colonies for a man with my wealth would be tolerable and from stories that I had heard there would be the opportunity to increase it manyfold. I had no doubt that at some time in the future things would settle down again in my home country and when the time was judged to be right I would return to the house that I had left behind in Versailles. I finally emerged from below decks into the daylight. The rocking of the vessel in the strong winds, even though it was tied up to the quayside, had left me feeling slightly queasy which certainly didn't bode well for the passage ahead.

* * *

Blinking, I stepped out just as Captain Jones arrived, issuing commands to all around him as he walked. Jones had been a sea Captain for the last ten years carrying goods back and forth between the French speaking lands of Florida in the south of the Colonies and the ports on the Atlantic coast of France. He rarely carried passengers as his strongly felt view was that they were rarely worth the trouble that they caused. It had cost me nearly double the going rate to persuade him that I would not even be noticed for the duration of the crossing. We had met several times in order to negotiate the details of the passage and although he would never admit it, I guessed that part of the consideration was that the Captain actually looked forward to some scholarly company and was of the opinion that it would help to pass some of the time. At this moment though, he was feeling aggrieved after a meeting with the port authority had increased the port tax that he was due to pay before departure. As a result those around him had felt the sharpness of his tongue as he expressed dissatisfaction with the speed with which his ship was being prepared for departure the following day. The news that he had received from the boatswain after stepping on board had done nothing to improve his temper. An American by birth he considered the foolishness by which France was tearing itself apart nothing to do with him whatsoever. His only interest was in making a good profit for the shipowners and of course, for himself. A wounded man was not good for business. It could present complications and worse, it could prevent him from leaving at all.

'Good day Captain. It's a fine morning.' I decided to take the lighthearted approach as though nothing had gone amiss. It didn't work.

* * *

'What in hell's name do you think that you are doing bringing a wounded man aboard my ship without my permission - which, incidentally, I would never have given.'

I continued in the same tone.

'A mere scratch to a friend of mine and you were not here to ask.'

'A mere scratch? I'm told that the man was within hours of losing his arm. The wound was going bad and it's fortunate for him that I have one of the best ship's doctors on either side of the Atlantic with me. I hope for his sake that you have made arrangements ashore for him. We sail in the morning as planned. These port leeches are costing me a fortune. People's tax. Ridiculous.'

Thinking quickly, I played my trump card.

'My friend Guillot will be too ill to move then but I think that I can help you with your financial worries. Hear me out please. He was planning on travelling to Bordeaux and he has a lot of money with him. Well - let's call it wealth. If you were prepared to make a slight detour via that port, I am sure that he would pay you well and the extra few days would help him to recover sufficiently.'

I was not sure if this would be the case but it would certainly be a lot better than abandoning him to his fate here in Rouen.

Captain Jones stopped and thought for a moment. 'Wealth you say? And what sort of wealth would that be?'

'Guillot is a wealthy merchant who trades in fine jewellery.

He has in his possession a selection of the finest diamond and gold bracelets and brooches. It would be a sacrifice for him but I am sure that he would be willing to trade some of these in order to obtain your help.'

The Captain listened carefully and thought again before speaking.

'Let us continue this conversation in my cabin and obtain a report from the doctor on your friend's condition. I will make my decision then.'

With that, he turned on his heel, dismissed his crew with instructions to make sure that all was prepared and stalked off leaving me to follow him as best I could.

Captain Jones didn't think of himself as a greedy man. He was aware however, that there were not many sea Captains that regularly traded across the Atlantic that lived extended and healthy lives. His plan was to accumulate enough money to enable him to settle down on land in the country of his birth as soon as was feasibly possible. Scurvy, dysentery and malaria were frequent killers and although he was one of the enlightened few, who attempted to keep them at bay by enforcing extra cleanliness and better fresh food for his crew, he was aware that it was only a matter of time before one or more struck his vessel.

We ducked into the Captain's cabin and sat to wait for the doctor or at least his assistant to appear with more information. We didn't have long to wait before there was a tap on the door and on command a youth in his late teens walked in. Nervously, he looked at the two of us waiting for confirmation that the Captain wanted him to speak.

* * *

'Begging your pardon sir but the Doctor told me to report to you whilst he deals with the gentlemen's wounds. He says that it is starting to go bad but if he removes the lead ball and keeps it washed and clean for a few days, all should be well.'

The boy was dismissed and the door closed.

'I suggest that as soon as it is finished you retrieve the belongings of your companion. I trust my crew as much as any Captain can but wealth such as you describe might be too much of a temptation. As far as passage goes, I am prepared to detour via Bordeaux but it will cost. I am guessing that the pistol wound is the result of trouble that you would rather avoid so in fact, by taking the two of you aboard now, I am endangering my voyage. My price will reflect this. I want the equivalent in payment of a four man passage to Florida. There will be no negotiation and I will decide on the value of any jewellery that you wish to use for payment.'

I would have agreed to any terms that were demanded, particularly as it was Guillot's possessions that I was using for the trade and so I quickly and readily agreed to the impositions made.

'I will call in on your doctor and retrieve the belongings of my friend. I then need to arrange for my trunk to be sent here. I will need to go into the town for several hours but I will be back before evening.'

Obtaining directions to the surgery, I left the Captain and made my way unsteadily along the decks until I reached my destination. I opened the door and was met by a sight that was as bloody as it was gloomy. Explaining the purpose of my call, I retrieved the bundle that had been dropped into one corner and quickly departed. Once back on deck it was only a matter of moments to establish the presence of a bag that was filled with the most exquisite objects. Jewellery that had belonged to Queen Marie Antoinette was now in the hands of a one time friend of the late Robespierre. How ironic.

The boy was still stood on the quayside patting my horse and after a few coins were passed on, I swung my leg over the saddle and slowly started to circumnavigate the crowds that were continuing to fill the area. It was only as I moved into the passageway that led into the town that I was startled to see a face that I recognised. A face that I really did not want to see.

3

In the hope that I hadn't been noticed I dismounted and led my horse through the crowds. The man had been looking the other way at the moment that I saw him and so I was hopeful that my presence had not been detected. But what on earth was he doing here?

I concentrated on putting some distance between us before mounting again and directing my horse towards my destination. My cousin's house was on the outskirts of the town where he was a successful merchant making a profitable living from the cargos that were brought into the harbour and then needed to be carted across to Paris. I had explained the need to temporarily store a trunk with him and my cousin had deliberately asked no questions.

'The less I know, the fewer lies I need to invent' was his only laconic comment. It did not take long for arrangements to be made to have the trunk taken to the ship later that afternoon and with a brief goodbye, I was on my way once more.

'Good morning Citizen Lestrade.'

I was as startled at the use of my formal title being so twisted as by the fact that I had been addressed by a figure that stood previously unseen in a passageway to my left. Inwardly groaning I stopped and heavily climbed down from my horse.

Nicholas De La Motte was a waster and a drunkard but when sober he had an evil streak and he always seemed to have funds to throw around. His presence here in Rouen could be no accident and despite my hopes that I had slipped by, I had obviously been followed from the quayside.

We had first met nine years earlier during what had become known as 'The Diamond Necklace Affair' - a miserable escapade that ultimately led to the downfall of Queen Marie Antoinette and that was despite her denial of any knowledge whatsoever of the machinations that had taken place, supposedly in her name.

De La Motte had been at the centre of the conspiracy and had always held me accountable for the fact that he had not profited from all of his artifice.

'And what, Citizen De La Motte, can I do for you, so far away from your usual haunts?'

I had known of instances where a person had been tried and executed for using the traditional Monsieur rather than the newly demanded title of Citizen. I was careful to give no cause for a complaint to be made against me.

I didn't like the expression on De La Motte's face as he replied. 'Not that you will, but you could speed things along by confirming my presumptions. I like to keep my ear to the ground and Paris is a small place for people of our ilk. When I heard that you had been backwards and forwards to Rouen earlier this month I started to wonder why. Then when I was watching your house in Versailles, there was an almighty ruckus with cries of a grand theft having taken place at the Petit Trianon, the late Queen's summer house. When I then called upon you only to be told that you were absent, it was my guess that you were involved in the theft and that Rouen was your destination. I rode furiously here just in time to see you carrying an obviously wounded figure aboard that vessel. I have to assume that it was the thief Guillot and that he was wounded during your escape. You have been noted for keeping unsavoury company. In fact, I wonder if it is my duty to inform the town guard of your presence here. I am sure that they would be delighted to delay the sailing and arrange for the two of you to be taken back to Paris for questioning.

I knew my adversary too well to think that this was what De La Motte really wanted and so I cautiously asked him.

The smirk on his face before he spoke was all too revealing. 'Well, since you mention it, my silence could certainly be bought. I know that despite the stories that you concocted on her behalf, Madam Deficit was the ultimate benefactor of the necklace that I worked so hard to obtain. Since her demise at the guillotine I would guess that it was taken by you or your friend during the theft.'

* * *

My mind went back to the furore that had surrounded the whole business. It was a complicated plot devised by the man in front of me together with his wife to defraud one of the biggest jewellers in France. In order to persuade them to gather the diamonds that were required and then to craft them into the most exquisite necklace, Madame De La Motte had spent months in gaining the trust of the Cardinal de Rohan. The Cardinal was desperate to regain the Queen's favour and as such had been easy to dupe. The crown jewellers Bohem and Bassange insisted that they had sold the necklace to the Queen using the Cardinal as an intermediary. The Queen, however, denied all knowledge or involvement. She detested the Cardinal so why would she use him at all? Rohan claimed that he had letters from the Queen, including her signature, which instructed him to act on her behalf. It was a strange business that had been choreographed by Madame De La Motte and her husband. It had all gone sour however, when the necklace had disappeared and no payments having been made, caused the jewellers to go out of business. The populace blamed Marie Antoinette despite her protestations of innocence. In fact, I had been called in to advise the Queen, a move that was unprecedented. My advice led to a campaign to calm the storm that had erupted throughout the country. She had claimed her innocence with me but had wanted someone with a knowledge of the people to help her to calm things down. My past history had forced me to agree to the arrangement but in all truth, I was never convinced that she was as innocent as she had claimed and now the evidence of her guilt was hidden in my house in Versailles. Amongst the jewellery that Guillot had stolen from the summer palace, it was the infamous necklace that he had happily handed over to me in exchange for my knowledge regarding the internal layout of the rooms.

* * *

I was certain that Madame De la Motte had become the Cardinal's lover in order to gain his trust and that with the knowledge and agreement of her husband. It was an indication of how serious these threats were. If he was prepared to countenance that arrangement, he was seriously determined to regain an artefact that he believed was rightly his.

'So let us be clear. I give the necklace to you and there will be no move on your part to warn the town council?'

'I assume that the necklace is on board the ship, in which case you will meet me after dark. The archway down to the quayside, where I know that you saw me earlier, is where I will be waiting at midnight. If you try to betray me, you will not be going anywhere tomorrow except back to Paris.'

The rest of the journey back to the ship was untroubled and it was not long afterwards that my trunk arrived containing not only everything that I needed for the journey but also much of my wealth. I had found that Guillot had been ensconced in my cabin and was lying awake although very weak.

'It sounds as though I need to thank you for saving my life. It also appears that I am to accompany you as far as Bordeaux although it will be an uncomfortable journey with two of us in this tiny cabin.'

The thief had readily accepted the fact that he would be unable to have the strength to make his own way before the departure of the vessel and had resigned himself to the journey through the Bay of Biscay.

* * *

'I am guessing that you have used some of the trinkets in my pack to pay for the journey?'

He flinched when I told him the actual cost of the voyage but acknowledged that there had been no other choice. 'I have plenty more in Bordeaux and there is still wealth aplenty that is waiting to be liberated.'

We talked about the events of the day and Guillot's enforced arrival in Rouen and then I decided to share with him the conversation that I had earlier had with De La Motte.

'You say that he wants the necklace that I gave you but that you have hidden it back in your house in Versaille?'

'That is the case. It seemed that it was judicious not to be caught with such an object in my possession. In any case, it is also my intention to return one day and it will be waiting for my arrival'.

Guillot was feeling light headed through loss of blood and so he assumed that this was the reason for him not being able grasp some of the things that he was being told.

'And you never explained to me how a lawyer of the people, a friend of Maximilien Robespierre who was feared by the Monarchy, was intimate with the rooms and chambers of the Queen's Summer Palace of Petit Trianon.'

'Well - we have much time to kill before I go to buy off De La Motte so I will tell you the tale of a misspent youth. Mine. Before I was twenty years of age I lived in Paris whilst training in the law. It was then that I met Maximilien and we became good friends. However, I also met another man, a certain Hans Axel von Fersen. He was a Swedish soldier who was a favourite of Marie Antoinette whilst she was still just the Dauphine. It is not well known but she was an inveterate gambler at this time and was extremely adept at the card game lansquenet. She invariably played for gold pieces and her chambers became a haunt for cardsharps and professional gamblers. Whilst studying in Paris, I also haunted the gambling dens that were rife within the City and became quite adept at the game. One night I had all but cleaned up the table at which I was sat when one of the fellows who had lost heavily all night begged a favour from me. He was out of funds but promised to repay me the following day. In return for the favour he promised to introduce me to the card tables at Le Petit Trianon. This man was the Queen's favourite Von Fersen. Now I say that the Queen's addiction to gambling was little known amongst the general population but there were rumours amongst the gamblers of Paris, although those that were introduced to Versaille were sworn to secrecy. If the King had found out how his new bride spent her time there, I dread to think of the possible consequences.

In the months and years that followed I secretly spent a lot of time there making a not inconsiderable amount of money in the process. I came to the attention of the Queen and she knew me by name. This is how I came to know the layout of the chambers and was able to describe them to you with such accuracy. It was also the reason that I was called upon to help to try to defuse the scandal that became known as the 'Affair of the Diamond Necklace'. A qualified lawyer by that time, a man of the people but on speaking terms with the Queen of France. A real mongrel but I could not let it be leaked that I was on such close terms with Royalty. My credibility would have disappeared overnight and as things turned out, I could easily have lost my head by now. She agreed to preserve my anonymity for any advice that I could give her. As it turned out, my advice was worthless because I am sure that this was the start of the murmurings that ultimately led to her demise.'

I glanced down to notice that at some point Guillot had dozed off. I took the opportunity to leave the cabin and track down first Captain Jones to confirm the time of sailing in the morning and then the Doctor to listen to his opinion on the wounds of my friend. 'All went well. I was able to extract the musket ball and clean all of the wounds. He has lost a lot of blood and so will be extremely weak for a number of days but I am optimistic for his recovery.'

Feeling much relieved, I returned quietly to the cabin and took the opportunity to update my journal. As was fashionable at the time I had been keeping a record of my day to day activities for a number of years and had much to write about the occurrences of the previous few days. It was growing dark by the time I had finished and so I lit a candle and spent the remaining few hours before the rendezvous, reading quietly. Guillot's sleep seemed untroubled which I took to be a positive sign of his impending recovery.

As midnight approached I slipped away. I was dreading the forthcoming meeting and I was unsure how De la Motte would react when he was offered an alternative to the necklace that he so dearly craved. The winds that had been blowing all day had increased in strength and the crew that kept watch were wrapped in their warmest clothing. The noise as it blew through the rigging was unearthly and it unsettled me even more. However, if we were to depart as planned in the morning, I had to persuade this loathsome man that it would not be worth his while to alert the guard. Even as we approached midnight there was still fervent activity as cargo was being loaded onto the ships around us. The sky was heavy with cloud and so the only light was from torches which had been soaked in wood tar. As I made my way across to the archway where we had agreed to meet, it was obvious that it would be too busy to carry out any kind of transaction. I touched the pack that I carried beneath my cloak and hoped that the wealth that it contained would be enough.

De La Motte stepped out of the shadows and brusquely spoke. 'Well? Do you have it?'

A horse drawn cart rattled by, closely followed by a group of sailors. 'Not here. There are too many prying eyes.'

I looked around and noticed an area of the quayside that was in darkness. Without waiting for an answer I simply said, 'Follow me' and then turned away striding towards the shadows. De La Motte followed but as we entered an area behind a stack of barrels, he pulled me by my shoulder and demanded again, 'Do you have it?'

'Not with me. It is hidden elsewhere. However, I can offer you these instead.'

I took out the pack and unwrapped a small fortune in gold pieces and diamond brooches. I had assembled it from some of my own wealth combined with the some of the remaining contents of my companions stolen property.

De La Motte actually snarled. It was a sound not unlike that uttered by a wild animal and then he struck me across the face. I staggered back, conscious of the long drop into the water behind me. Regaining my balance I tried to persuade him. He was not receptive and attacked again. Street fighting was not within my repertoire of skills and it was obvious that I had little chance against the ferocious anger that confronted me. He struck me again and again so before I succumbed I reached into the pack and quickly pulled out a dagger that was decorated with silver and pearl. It was a decorative piece but lethal looking nonetheless. For the first time since it had been crafted it found its way between the ribs of a man. I pulled it back out and stabbed again. Just at that moment the clouds exposed enough of the moon for me to see the look of utter astonishment on my opponent's face as he realised what had happened. He staggered, first one way and then the other and as he swayed, I pushed hard. The splash as his body entered the water below us was barely audible in the howling wind. I was breathing heavily, gasping for breath but I had the presence of mind to launch the dagger into the water after him. Our activities had not been noticed and so once I recovered myself, I made my way back.

I finished telling the story to Guillot who had been awake upon my return and paused to hear his opinion of the night's events.

'And you are sure that he had no companion?' he asked.

'No. From the way that he spoke and acted, I am certain that he was alone.'

'In that case, you have probably done the world a favour. I would think no more about it. It might be wise to get some sleep whilst we are still tied up. Once underway tomorrow, there will be no sleep for anyone until this storm has blown itself out.' In his injured state, my friend was quick to take his own advice but I found sleep more difficult to come by. I had little conscience about the demise of De La Motte, particularly in these times when life was so cheaply thought of. I was more anxious to see the ship leave port unhindered in the morning. It would only be then that I would be able to relax. It was hours later that I drifted off into a restless slumber.

4

I was abruptly woken by the sound of voices shouting loudly. For a moment I thought that my deeds of the previous night had been discovered but then I realised that the sounds that I could hear were the sounds of a vessel being readied for departure. It was daylight and I had no idea how long I had been asleep. Guillot was not in his berth so I blinked to clear my eyes and made my way outside. I had been mistaken. It had not been the sound of a vessel being readied, but in fact a vessel that had actually departed. The coastline could be seen behind us, but the thing that was most noticeable, this time being my first out at sea, was the movement of the boat. Whether this was normal or a product of the ever increasing wind I did not know, but it was a frightening experience to see the horizon rolling up and down. I had guessed that Guillot had been taken for attention by the doctor and it seemed to me that I had slept for the devil as I had not heard a thing until just a few minutes ago. The surgery then would be my first destination, that is, if I were able to negotiate the deck that rolled and pitched and swayed making walking almost impossible for me. What made it worse was the nausea that I was starting to feel in my stomach - I had heard of sea sickness - mal de mer - and the description had not been exaggerated. Cautiously, hanging on to any rope or railing that I could find I made my way slowly to the area where I had seen my friend the previous day. I hoped that the condition of his wounds would not be such that my stomach would want to evacuate its contents, but on entering I found him sat on a chair whilst the good doctor was washing his hands in the corner of the room. They greeted me warmly and I was pleased to hear that all was well. No infection had set in and it was now simply a matter of time until he would be fully recovered. I asked Doctor Shaw about my stomach and when he had finished laughing, he offered me no optimism for the forthcoming journey. He was also pessimistic about the developing storm.

'From what I hear it could turn out to be one of the worst in many years. You are lucky that the Captain holds to his word because the delay caused by our little detour to Bordeaux could be costly. He would prefer to outrun it across the Atlantic rather than hug the coastline for the next few days. My advice is to stay in your berth - both for the sake of your stomach but also to avoid Captain Jones's irritation. Let him take it out on the crew.'

I offered to help my friend back to our cabin and fully intended to take the counsel that I had just been given. The return journey was even worse than my arrival as Guillot was very weak and unsteady on his feet. He was exhausted when we finally arrived and collapsed onto his berth without saying a word. I looked around the gloomy cabin and spent the next few minutes tidying the mess created by two men, as much as I could. I had been described as fastidious before but I was used to being looked after by my servants and the mess that had crept upon us in the last day or so was not to my liking. I looked forward to leaving Guillot at his destination and recovering the space for myself. The rest of the day passed slowly, much of it in conversation with my friend. Any barriers that there had been between us had disappeared and he opened his soul to me like a long lost brother. Some of his story I already knew. He had been born as an aristocrat - in fact into one of the wealthiest families in France. As he grew older, he became more and more aware of the massive gulf that existed between his life and that of the Parisian peasants. He told me of the day that his father had chosen to throw food scraps to a starving dog rather than the starving child by its side. I had heard stories about the dangers of standing in the street if his father approached. He would ride over someone rather than go round them and then lash at them with his riding whip for the impertinence of being ahead of him. As he approached his coming of age, Guillot was determined to put right some of the misdoings of his family. The only way that he knew was to take pieces of family jewellery and sell them, giving the proceeds to the downtrodden. Of course, he was soon caught, cruelty was the family characteristic not stupidity and he was grievously beaten. Not only that, it was decided that he should be cast out to make his own way in the world. Untrue stories about him were spread by his family so that no one in his circle would help or even speak to him. He was physically manhandled by the family servants and deposited in the dust outside his home. His father watched dispassionately and before he turned to go back through the gates, he pulled a ring off his finger and with the words, 'This is your inheritance. You are no longer a member of this family', threw the gold and amethyst item at Guillot's feet.

'That was the last time that I saw him. It was ten years ago but it has been an expensive ten years for him and his ilk. I'm afraid that the Parisian poor were the real losers as from that day forward I needed to make my own way. I sold the ring immediately and was able to find comfortable lodgings while I formulated my plans. It was easy to break into the houses that I had known so well and take the choicest pieces. It soon became impossible to sell them in the city though and so after each foray, I would make my way down to Bordeaux and there adopted the life of a respectable merchant. I could sell what I chose and was soon able to buy a house and then invest in land. I own many vineyards in the area that are managed by people that I trust. Truth be told I could have moved there and lived an honest life quite comfortably. The trouble is, I really enjoyed taking my revenge on Parisian society. I could feel their fear and mistrust in each other.'

'So what next?' I asked. 'Are you planning to return to your life in Paris after you have recovered?'

'I will see. This brush with death has startled me somewhat. Maybe it is a sign that the time has come to settle down to an honest life.'

He sighed. 'I would miss the action though.'

The next two days were spent in a similar vein with long conversations being interspersed with visits from the doctor and me taking the air as best I could on the wildly rolling deck. The shore was no longer visible but after two days I was assured that we were currently crossing the Bay of Biscay running parallel to the French coastline. Nantes and then La Rochelle were passed by but then soon afterwards I could feel a change in the direction of the howling wind and I was told that we were making directly for Bordeaux. I would be sorry to see the last of my companion but infinitely delighted to stop for a few hours on a land that didn't pitch and heave. By now the sky was getting blacker and although it was only midday it was as dark as dusk. The shoreline soon came into view, first as a thin line on the horizon but soon more and more detail could be seen. As we approached the shore once more the movement of the boat lessened until we finally entered the mouth of the Garonne river and eventually found a berth at the busy quayside. The decision was taken by the Captain to return to sea immediately after dropping off my friend. Even in his weakened state he reassured me that his home was only minutes away and that he would be able to summon immediate assistance. Heartened by these comments we said our goodbyes and I helped him with the remnants of his pack down on to the quay. Within minutes of my return the vessel was once again making its way down the river, this time to the open sea, with a long and arduous voyage to the American Colonies ahead of us. As we left the river mouth and moved out into the bay the movements of the ship noticeably increased and I decided that it would be more comfortable to spend the next few hours in my cabin hoping that the further that we sailed into the Atlantic the more that the storm would decrease.

As the day wore on the movements of the clipper became more and more violent. I have to say that I hardly noticed as the sickness that overcame me voided my insides and left me weak and shaking. The noise of the vessel creaking and banging competed with the howling of the wind which was becoming louder and louder. At one point the Doctor appeared to check on my wellbeing and also carrying news of our progress. It seems that this storm was the most violent that he had ever seen on this side of the Atlantic and it almost compared with some of those that ripped into the Southern States of the American Colonies. Our progress was being hampered and we were slowly but inexorably being swept southwards towards the Spanish and Portuguese coasts. No matter how hard they had tried, the crew were unable to make any westerly progress and Captain Jones had eventually decided to try to run before the storm and hope that it would blow itself out. My misery was compounded by the news and I fiercely wished that I had never planned this escape. How I would survive a voyage of several weeks was beyond me although I was reassured that seasickness was a temporary condition and that most people overcame it sooner or later. I succumbed to sleep once more and slumbered fitfully for what seemed to be days. There were no signs of this tempest abating and each time that I awoke I could hear shouts that seemed evermore frantic. The next time that the good doctor appeared he looked drawn and worried and the news that he carried wasn't good. The mast had suffered significant damage and as a result it was necessary to find shelter and make repairs. By now we were running down the Portuguese coast and Porto which lay on the Douro river was within reach. It had been decided to dock there until the vessel was made seaworthy again.

What was bad news for the Captain and crew came as a blessing to me and my spirits rose at the thought of stepping onto land again so soon. Once again the movement started to abate as we neared the shore and as we approached the mouth of the river I ventured on deck, partly to escape the stench in my cabin and partly to see what new horizons awaited us. I had heard of Porto although I had never before ventured into Portugal. It was said that it was partly populated by English merchants who made a good living exporting the local wine, which had been fortified with spirits in order to keep it from going sour on it's journey to England. The river was wide as it entered the sea and Porto itself was just a short distance inland. Eventually, ropes and hawsers were thrown ashore and tied up. The Doctor had not exaggerated about the state of the mainmast and although it remained in place a large split could clearly be seen. The men who had taken down the sail in the midst of the boiling sea and howling wind were heroes in my eyes although I was told that this was just the expectation of the job that they had. I found Captain Jones and after a jocular exchange regarding the state of my health, I learned that repairs would not be carried out quickly and that I was welcome to find lodgings ashore for the duration. This appealed to me far more than the thought of that wretched stinking cabin and so I stepped on to dry land for the first time in many days. My first concern was in making myself understood. I spoke passable English but I had no knowledge of the Portuguese language whatsoever. However, in the first tavern that I encountered, I came across a group of English merchants who reassured me that their mother tongue was widely understood throughout the town. They also gave me the address of a house where I should be able to find lodgings that were comfortable enough to tide me by during my enforced stay. It was only minutes away and I was fortunate enough to find that there was one room available. It was large and clean with a bed to one side and a writing table and chair below a window that looked out across the harbour. More to the point it had a strong looking lock which was of great importance to me. I could not risk leaving my trunk unattended on board the ship for it contained the majority of my wealth. As I stepped outside, heading back to collect my belongings the sun emerged from behind the clouds for the first time in what seemed to be many weeks. This combination of safety, dry land and sunshine made me happier than I had been for a long time. This Portuguese city was welcoming me it seemed.

The trunk was heavy and I needed the help of a cart and driver that I was able to commandeer to get it up to my new lodgings. It was starting to get dark when I finally felt myself to be settled and my stomach was complaining at its lack of content. Time to find some food. The landlady directed me towards a nearby 'taberna' that she highly recommended and by the time that I had eaten and returned I was feeling exhausted. The journey had taken its toll. I slept well that night.

The next few days passed quickly. The clouds had rolled away, the sky was blue and it was warm. I spent the time exploring this old town and talking to anyone that I could get to listen. Not only had the English descended to make their fortune in the wine trade but a number of my own countrymen had made their way here to see what could be learned from the Portuguese wine growers. It was a cosmopolitan atmosphere that I enjoyed very much. I paid several visits to the ship and spent one very unpleasant afternoon cleaning up the mess that I had left in my cabin. Captain Jones was very insistent that I did not use any of his crew for the task. It was after I had returned to the quayside and decided to walk along the river bank out to the coast that I had one of those moments of clarity that occur once in a while. My intention had been to escape to the American Colonies in order to avoid the inevitable consequences of staying in Paris and Versailles. Fortuitously I now found myself in exactly that situation. I was in a city that was safe but that boasted an excellent climate. Although I spoke no Portuguese I was able, in most situations, to be able to make myself understood. I liked the food and wine well enough and with blinding clarity I realised that I was dreading the voyage across the Atlantic. Those few days in the storm were more than enough for me and I could not envisage how I would manage far out at sea if another struck the boat whilst I was aboard. The solution was blindingly simple. Obtain a house here and make my life amongst the Portuguese and English until France had come to its senses and it was safe to return. There were business opportunities aplenty even if I could not practice my profession. I immediately turned on my heels and marched back to the vessel. I think that Captain Jones was relieved that he would not have to nursemaid me for the following weeks and of course he kept the money that he had been paid. I said my goodbyes to him and the doctor and in a much happier frame of mind made my way back to the lodging house where I was staying. The landlady was a kind soul and was more than happy for me to stay with her until such time that I had found a place of my own. One of my first tasks when I had arrived had been to find a broker in order to sell a gold ring in order to obtain some local coinage. I had most of that left but I suspected that the man had not been totally fair with me. Perhaps it was time to compare his honesty with that of some of his competitors. Also, there was the matter of my trunk. It was heavy and it was locked but the sooner it was away from a rented room and into a more secure place of safety, the more relaxed I would become.

And so I went to look for a house. In comparison to Paris, Porto was cheap. Food, drink and housing cost a fraction of what I was used to paying. As a result, within a matter of days, I was able to take out a long lease on a merchant's townhouse which was situated in a district known as the Ribeira which I believe refers to its proximity to the river. The merchant in question had decided to return to England and was delighted to find a tenant to take on the house - particularly one who would pay for twelve months in advance. I lost no time in moving my belongings once again and I was soon settled into the large townhouse which had glorious views across the wide river Douro. There were many rooms - most of which I would simply shut up and not use. Those that faced the river though were large light and airy. All that remained was to find a way of gainfully occupying my time.

It was two months later to the day that I found myself, three hundred kilometres away in the capital city of Lisbon, crouched behind a garden wall. The first musket shot was well wide but the next splintered a stone just above my head.

5

In my younger days I had frequently been characterised as 'headstrong' by those who knew me well. It was a trait that had landed me in many scrapes but had also led to some of my most interesting experiences. Without it, I cannot imagine that I would ever have been seen playing cards at the Queen's tables or even been involved in the 'Affair of the Queen's Necklace'. It was also the reason that my friend Robespierre did not recommend me to the Council. But to put a different spin on things, he is extremely dead and I am very much alive. This was a state of affairs however, that would only continue as long as I could get away from these musket balls that were shattering stone and rock around me. Having loaded my own weapon, I decided that it was time to unleash a shot in the direction of my pursuers. I had no hope of hitting anyone in the dark but it did have the effect of making them more reluctant to hurry in their pursuit of me.

They actually had no need to hurry. I was going nowhere and dawn would arrive in due course. If I had not left this place by then my soul was destined to meet that of my late friend. I needed to do some serious thinking.

I took the opportunity of a lull in the fusillade to get a quick look around. The house that I had just left was situated a few hundred metres in front of me. I was hiding behind a stone wall which I had tumbled over in the dark whilst running wildly away from several armed and angry men. My understanding of the Portuguese language had improved slightly since arriving in Porto and I was well able to hear words being shouted that I translated as 'thief' and 'death'. Not a good situation to be in. It was a dark night but the open field behind me ran for a clear hundred metres and there was no chance that I could clear it without being seen.

'And it was your fault that I was in that situation.'

I looked across at my friend Guillot then stood to place another log on the fire. It crackled as it burnt and threw sparks up the chimney into the night air. Even Porto could be cold in October. Soon after I had settled I had written to him in Bordeaux explaining that I had decided to stay here and so it was only a few months before I was honoured with a visit. Many vessels plied their trade up and down this coast and so obtaining passage from Bordeaux to Porto was relatively simple if not a little expensive. As I was to find out, he had taken a slightly unorthodox way of travelling. He had recovered well and it was difficult to tell whether his good humour was the result of the Port wine that we were drinking or the tale of woe that I was relating.

'How so?' he replied. 'I knew nothing of your whereabouts

or your doings at this time.'

'After I had settled here, I looked for something that would occupy my time. My understanding of the Portuguese language was poor and the English were not going to let a Frenchman into their wine trade. Then I thought of you and wondered if the odd escapade might relieve the boredom. I chose Lisbon as my target because of the excess of wealth that resides there as well as the fact that it is far enough away from here to allow me to retreat home after a foray. The first time went well. I was in and out without detection and was able to sell my gains here for a good profit. The second time was more exciting. Like you at the Trianon in Versailles, it was a dog that heard me and started barking. That brought the staff running with their pistols.'

'So, pinned down behind a wall. No hope of escape. How did you get away? I am intrigued.'

My story was going down well so I paused for a few moments to replenish the glasses and allow the tension to build. The situation in which I had found myself was quite ludicrous but my escape had actually been quite simple.

'As I crouched behind the wall, a gap opened in the clouds and I was able to see more clearly. A few metres away there was an open ditch running away into the distance. As soon as it darkened again I let loose another shot to persuade them to keep their heads down then wriggled my way to safety. What frustrated me the most however, was the fact that I made no profit. I was forced to run before taking anything of value.'

By this point Guillot was roaring with laughter. Eventually, he was able to gulp enough air to speak. 'If you are going to take on a life of crime, you must be prepared for setbacks. However, if they occur every other time you go out I would suggest that your life expectancy is somewhat limited.'

This set him off again and only a large gulp from his glass was able to quiet the laughter.

'I would also suggest, my friend, that you look to other pursuits and leave this life of thievery behind in its infancy. In fact I am seriously considering the same myself. I have proposed marriage and been accepted by a merchant's daughter by the name of Susanna. She and I have known each other for some while and I thought that it was time that I settled down. The businesses that I have built in Bordeaux will be more than enough to occupy my time. She is a sweet thing and has no knowledge of my alternative occupation.'

I shouted my congratulations and hugged my friend closely. That night we drank more wine than was good for us.

The following morning our heads were sore but we took a walk along the riverside to try to clear the alcohol fumes that still resided within. Guillot pointed out a coastal vessel that was berthed a little way along. With some pride he told me that it partly belonged to him and that he was making a tidy profit in transporting and selling goods between France, Spain and Portugal.

'And I don't even smuggle the contents. I pay the full taxes due and I am able to sleep easy as an honest and responsible citizen.'

'So you are serious about changing your ways and settling

down?' I asked.

'Very serious. I am making more money now by plying an honest trade than I ever did in thievery. I will miss the excitement but I think that the good people of Paris will be relieved. But what about you? It must be desperate times if you are looking to a life of crime to relieve the tedium.'

'Not desperate, but as I can not practise as a lawyer in this country, I must find something to occupy my time. I tried to take an interest in the wine trade from the Douro Valley but the English have it all tied up and they are not going to let a Frenchman move in. Hence my extramural interests.'

Guillot listened carefully to what I was saying then quietly replied, 'If I were you I would put up with the tedium for a little longer. From what I hear, things are starting to change back home. There is movement within the People's Committee and a new, fresh face is showing his strength. His name is Bonaparte and he hails from Corsica. If the changes continue at the present rate, France will be a different country within a year or two. Who knows, it might be safe for you to travel back again.'

He paused before continuing, this time with a big smile on his face, 'But not of course if you are dead in Porto.'

Later that day we said our goodbyes and promised to stay in touch by mail that could be carried by the Captain of Guillot's ship that would be running up and down the coast.

I spent the next few days thinking about my prospects here in Portugal. Porto was a fine city but it was becoming increasingly obvious that it was not going to occupy me for long. I had been hearing stories about events in Lisbon and the nearby town of Sintra that intrigued me and decided that the time had arrived to temporarily move my belongings further south to Lisbon itself. In particular, I had listened to merchants gossiping about an English nobleman by the name of William Beckford who had recently rented an estate close to Sintra. He was said to be both eccentric and extremely wealthy and I was keen to make his acquaintance as soon as possible. My experience in Paris throughout the years suggested that there was often a profit to be made from this particular combination.

And so it was, I found myself two months later, renting a house that was set just off the Praca do Comercio, a large square that had been built on the ruins of a royal palace that was destroyed in the earthquake some fifty years earlier. It was a bustling area and it was obvious why the square had been so named. It was surrounded by arched galleries where merchants plied their trade but it then opened at one end to the Tagus river where ships came and unloaded their cargo before reloading with fresh goods to take elsewhere. A busy place indeed but it was fascinating to watch and to listen to the myriad of tongues - some spoken in English or French which I understood but many more in languages that were strange to me.

I spent my time exploring the city which was new and vibrant, many of the buildings having been constructed recently as a consequence of the earthquake. One of my favourite districts was the Chiado neighbourhood which was rich with coffee houses and theatres and it was there that I discovered a bookshop that was frequented by expatriate Englishmen. Strangely, they seemed to spend much of their time sitting around a large table arguing about writers and poets rather than browsing the extensive stock that the shop contained. The owner, an elderly Portuguese, seemed not to mind and in fact encouraged them by frequently serving them coffee and port wine.

The exterior of the shop was covered in the blue tiles that were typical of the city. The inside consisted of a series of vaulted ceilinged rooms about which books were scattered in what seemed to me to be no particular order. Perhaps they were simply placed where a gap became available following a previous sale. It was during a heated debate about the events that had taken place in Paris during the previous years that I took the opportunity to intervene and introduce myself. I had been visiting the shop for a number of days and had become curious about the origins of this fluid group of gentlemen. Why were they there? What had led them to Lisbon and why did they spend so much of their time in this particular establishment.

Their current argument had been related to the rise of the Committee in Paris and the demise of my friend Robespierre. The discussion had become quite heated with one group favouring the execution without understanding the politics that had been behind the event. The other group had been arguing to the contrary but had been equally ill informed. As soon as I interjected and introduced myself they invited me to sit with them and listened carefully to my story. Several hours passed and as the flow of coffee decreased the intake of port wine increased proportionally. It seemed that they were a group of friends from England who had heard stories about the nearby town of Sintra and had made their way here independently as part of their European tour. One man in particular, they told me, this William Beckford of whom I had heard, had become so enamoured by the area he had negotiated the rental of an estate and intended to stay for several years. By the time the gathering had broken up it was becoming dark outside and I had been encouraged to join them again the following day.

The streets of Lisbon were illuminated by lamps burning a strange mixture of vegetable oils which gave off an unappealing aroma. This, combined with the smoky soot that was a byproduct of the flame, meant that I was seldom abroad after nightfall. It was also a time when some of the less desirable members of the society would emerge so I was not surprised when I sensed that I was being followed. Several times I looked back over my shoulder just in time to see a figure disappear into the shadows. I made a point of staying on the broader, better lit streets avoiding alleyways whenever possible. The roads in this part of the city are steep but fortunately, returning home was downhill so I was able to make good time. Before entering my house I checked carefully that there was no-one nearby and once inside I latched and locked the door carefully. It was solidly made of ancient oak and the bolts and locks were sturdy. I was home and I was safe.

Several days passed before I found myself in the Chiado district again and this time when I walked into the bookshop I was warmly greeted by my new friends and chided for not having joined them sooner. I learned that many of this group were acquaintances of William Beckford and were due to travel to Sintra to stay as his guest one week hence and they insisted that I came along as well. They told me that the house that came with the estate was large enough to easily accommodate them as well as myself and that Beckford encouraged visitors to this remote part of Portugal. I took little persuading to agree. The week flew by and I made a point of visiting the bookshop several more times even though Lisbon had many other wonders to discover. The enigmatic William Beckford was said to be extremely wealthy, eccentric to a degree and a writer of some note. His gothic novel Vathek, so I was told, had been well received in England. Fortunately it was available in the book store and I took the opportunity to purchase a copy.

I spent the following week reading this work of Beckford's and found it to be surprisingly palatable. What made it easier for me was the fact that he had written the original in French and it was this version that I had purchased. It was an Arabian tale but one that took on elements of a horror story with the appearance of ghosts and spirits. I read long into the night and filled my days with further exploration.

The day for departure was soon upon me and early that morning a carriage arrived outside my house containing two of the company and their baggage. As I left the house I happened to look down the street. I stopped, stunned for a moment by what I thought I had seen. Climbing into a carriage that was similar in appearance to the one that had just arrived for me was a man who was the image of a certain Nicholas De La Motte who currently resided at the bottom of the harbour in Rouen.

6

It took all day to ride to Sintra and I was uncommonly quiet throughout the journey. On the one hand I was certain of what I had seen; on the other, it was frankly impossible. De La Motte was dead. I had stabbed him myself and pushed his body into the water. When my companions queried my lack of humour, I simply told them that I was feeling a little hungover and that I would be fine in due course. That seemed to satisfy them and they continued their conversations about the towns and countries that they had visited since leaving England. All told there were three carriages travelling towards the hills so it seemed that Mr. Beckford was going to have a full house.

Eventually, we approached the town itself - a bustling, busy place that was dominated by the Royal Palace. The Palace is located in the centre of the town and can be seen from afar because of the two white, conical shaped chimneys that rise out from the kitchens. Behind the town the hills rise up to a high ridge along which marches the old Moorish walls. It was an exquisite place and popular with the Royal Family who used it as an escape from the heat of Lisbon. However, if gossip was to be believed, the Queen had not taken well to the recent deaths of her husband and eldest son and was currently known by the population as Maria the Mad.

The estate that had been taken by Mr. Beckford was a little way out of town so we paused for an hour in order to take some refreshment. The pastries of the area were famous and I had certainly taken a liking to them myself. As we sat and ate I noted that the population of the town was even more cosmopolitan than that of Lisbon. Sintra was gaining in fame and this was reflected by the number of visitors from across Europe that it was receiving. The time arrived to move on and so we piled ourselves back into the carriages and made our way up into the foothills. The road to the Monserrate Palace, for so our destination was named, was steep and narrow and the surrounding countryside seemed to spill down upon us with exotic bushes and trees. As we climbed steadily upwards we passed a number of estates and grand houses until eventually, we entered by the gate house of our destination and passed by a waterfall and a grand lake before seeing in front of us an exotic palatial villa. We had arrived.

We tumbled out of the carriages, dusty and hot from our long journey, to be met by one of Mr. Beckford's staff. He apologised for his master's absence but informed us that he was still exploring the gardens and would likely return soon enough. In the meantime he escorted us, in our bedraggled state, to the drawing room where we were served with tea. This is a peculiar English custom that I still find odd in the extreme. The room was large with chalky red coloured walls, the furnishings were grand and obviously carried some age. The views from the windows were stunning. We overlooked a terrace beyond which a lawn ran away into a lake which was surrounded by large and ancient trees. Beyond this the estate climbed upwards and I assumed that it was this area that our host was exploring, although how convoluted must it be if he were still making new discoveries months after taking tenancy.

I needed to stretch my legs and so I wandered out of the drawing room and down the corridor. An open door led into a most sumptuous library which contained ceiling high bookcases all around the room. The shelves were packed with books with only a very few spaces still unoccupied. The only relief to this wall of leather was at the far end where a large fireplace sat below two circular portraits. An interesting place indeed. I sat in a leather chair and took down a novel by Voltaire that I knew well. I thumbed through the book which had obviously been read far fewer times than my own copy at home in Versailles. After a little while I heard voices talking excitedly and so replacing the book I made my way back to join my friends.

William Beckford was holding court with everyone surrounding him. They had told me little about him but he obviously had left England following some kind of a scandal. As I walked into the room he stopped in mid sentence and turned towards me. I was warmly welcomed and he refuted my apologies simply saying that I should stay as long I wished. It appeared that he had an open house policy that saw a constant flow of visitors. He stood tall but with features that were, to my eyes, slightly effeminate. His clothes were as bedraggled as ours, a fact that he explained away by describing the rill and waterfall that he had just been tracing out on the estate. I was able to easily gain his approval by quoting from his novel Vathek that I had bought last week in Lisbon.

'A man of rare breeding and good taste,' he laughed and then repeated the phrase in my own French language in case I had not understood. I was to learn that this rich English gentleman was something of a polymath, being educated in a range of languages, philosophy, law, music and literature to name but a few. He was about my own age but came from a much more privileged background. I was also to learn more about the scandal that had driven him out of England - but that was still to come. For the moment I was happy with my situation having incorporated myself into the inner circle. I now needed to look for opportunities that I could turn to my financial advantage; nothing illegal, just a chance to swell my coffers. I could not practise my trade in the law for the time being so I needed to exercise my wits.

The rest of the day passed in something of a blur. I was shown to my room by one of the servants and left to bathe and dress myself in something more appropriate. Drinks were taken before we were all served with a sumptuous dinner. We were encouraged to tell our stories either of travelling around Europe or in my case escaping from the Revolution. Beckford was extremely skilled on the piano claiming to have been tutored at one point by no less a maestro than Wolfgang Mozart. His playing rounded off an enjoyable and memorable evening. We retired early that night after an exhausting day all round.

The next morning I rose early having been awoken by an extravagance of birdsong. My bedroom, like that of all the guests, was in the north tower and overlooked terracotta tiles and then bushes and trees as far as the eye could see. As soon as I was dressed I strolled out onto the lawn and walked down to the lake. This was to become a habit in the weeks that followed. Born and brought up in central Paris and only recently having moved to Versailles, the countryside was still a novelty to me. By the time that I returned to the house breakfast was ready and everyone had emerged. Beckford declared that he was going to spend the day on the estate but that we were welcome to enjoy the palatial comforts of his home and then meet him for dinner that evening.

I spent the morning exploring this sumptuous place starting in the octagonal entrance hall and making my way by stages to the beautiful music room at the furthest end. We had listened to Beckford playing compositions from masters such as Mozart and Haydn last night and to my untrained ears the acoustics were excellent. This room was decorated with friezes and plasterwork and situated in the middle was a large grand piano. The devil only knows how they managed to get it to this spot. It was the library however, to which I eventually migrated and spent the first of many happy hours amongst the shelves and books. Occasionally, I would walk outside to stretch my legs but the heat of the day soon drove me back inside. I sometimes came across my English companions and it was obvious that in varying degrees they were becoming restless already. More fool them I thought. They were accustomed to this wealth and luxury. For me, it was and would remain a dream that I planned to enjoy for as long as possible.

The weeks that followed continued in a similar pattern. Rising early with a walk down to the lake, followed by a day of reading interspersed with walks around the grounds. The season was changing and the leaves on the trees were beginning to adopt their autumnal colours. As a result the temperature was dropping and so my forays were becoming more wide ranging. I came to know the estate as well as any visitor was able and on a number of occasions was fascinated to come across Beckford and some of his staff. He was in the process of diverting a stream so that it would fall over a precipitous rock face creating a waterfall. He claimed that it would be more aesthetic like this and who was I to argue. A stone bridge was part completed which crossed the diverted stream and looked down on to the water tumbling down the sheer face. I had extended my pre breakfast walk so that I now strode past the ornamental lake and climbed the steep path to admire the view from here. Literature teaches us that an idyllic existence cannot continue for ever and so it proved with me.

The change came when I next visited the town of Sintra itself. I had agreed to join those of my English friends that still remained in a foray to explore this ancient and beautiful place. From a group of seven of us that had arrived a month ago, now only three remained and so we took just one carriage which was driven by a jovial native of the area. The road down was steep but he was skilled with the horses and made sure that they were secure in their footing and so we arrived without incident. The town itself was much quieter than when we had stopped en route from Lisbon. Summer was behind us and most of the visitors had gone, leaving behind just the permanent residents. The weather now was still much more clement than back home in Paris but on occasion, we had awoken to stupendous mists that blanketed the area. Today was one such day and Sintra being much lower down the valley than the estate where I was staying was eerie and mystical in its shroud. My friends immediately declared their desire to find a tavern but my preference was for further exploration. I parted from them agreeing a time when I would rejoin them in order to return. There were very few people about. Sinatra was a small town in any case and the weather had driven most of the population indoors. I enjoyed having the streets to myself and started out by exploring some of the steep alleyways that surrounded the Pena Palace. The dense mist muffled my footsteps and it was a delight to weave my way back and forth, turning a corner to find a view of the palace itself one minute and then up to the mist shrouded hillside the next. These lanes turned back on themselves and so it was possible to find that one unexpectedly emerged into a small square that had been passed five minutes earlier. And then it happened. The shock that I had experienced several weeks earlier when leaving Lisbon had slowly disappeared from my mind. I had convinced myself that I had been mistaken in identifying the person getting into the carriage as Nicholas De La Motte. I knew that he was dead. I had felt my knife grating on his ribs and I had seen him sink into the harbour in Rouen and yet on entering a church square that I had passed through several times already, there stood in front of me, was the man himself. This time it was no fleeting glance. He stood staring directly at me, smiling sardonically and then stepped out of sight. Foolishly I did not follow him. The shock made me turn in the opposite direction and walk away from the area as quickly as I could. How was it possible? The man had returned from the dead and it was obvious that he would be after one thing only. The Queen's necklace. De La Motte was obsessed. But why not? Even if it were broken up, the diamonds in the necklace would allow him to live in extraordinary luxury for the rest of his life. But it was puzzling. I had been foolish in admitting my knowledge of its whereabouts back in Rouen but how had the man escaped death and then followed me first to Lisbon and then here to Sintra. This affair was far from being finished. If De La Motte had followed me this far then he must know where I was staying. It was time to take precautions. Back in Paris, not being of the nobility or a soldier, I had not been allowed to carry a sword but in this less refined part of the world it was not uncommon for travellers to arm themselves for protection against footpads or highwaymen.

Back at the estate, later in the day, it quickly became clear to me that I was not going to be able to protect myself that easily. Carrying a fully primed pistol with me each time that I left the house was not an option. It was more likely to accidentally discharge and injure me than not. A sword was not the answer either. I had persuaded one of his fellow guests to give me a lesson in the art of swordsmanship and it quickly became obvious that against a man such as De La Motte, a fight of this nature would be short and fatal. Nor was a knife the answer. I had caught my assailant by surprise in Rouen but it would not be allowed to happen again. I needed another solution and it was back in the library that I surprisingly found one. Several days passed without me leaving the security of the house, most of the time spent thumbing through the myriad of books and journals that were shelved therein. It was a pamphlet titled, 'Self-Defense for Gentlemen' that provided the solution. The passage that caught my eye started with the sentence:

'Every gentleman should be able to protect himself from insult and violence.'

All of my obvious but disregarded solutions were discussed but then I read:

* * *

'As a queller of disturbances, I know nothing better than a hickory or ash stick, particularly if it is carried with a head that has been drilled and weighted with lead shot.'

With some fascination I continued to read how the author advocated the use of such a weapon and so it was, later that day, that I came to find myself in conversation with William Beckford and without describing the immediate fears that had led to the request, I asked if the requirements to construct such an implement lay to hand.

Beckford laughed heartily and simply pointed to a door that had been locked since my arrival. He produced a key from his waistcoat pocket and opened up a room that contained a veritable arsenal of weaponry. They were the remnants of a time before he arrived, he explained, when this was a dangerous and unlawful area. The owner of each estate took it upon himself to provide the means of protection for his servants. He reached below one of the benches and took out a walking stick that he handed to me saying, 'Take it and use it as you will. It is yours.'

I took the stick in my hand. It was exactly the right length for me to use in its primary function but the weight of the gnarled head was immediately noticeable.

'Give someone a biff with that and they will not be troubling you. Anyone in particular in mind?'

I took note of the astute question but simply blustered that no, it was just for general protection. And so it was that I resumed my walks around the estate, but now accompanied by what was, to all appearances, a substantial walking cane. The days passed pleasantly and reassured by my new gift I ventured further and further from the house. It was inevitable that De La Motte should show his face again and so it proved one damp and drizzly morning when I had taken my customary pre breakfast walk. I was standing on the newly completed bridge overlooking the dark waters of the artificially constructed waterfall when I sensed a presence in the trees. Sure enough, De La Motte appeared on the track just beyond the end of the bridge. A sword was in his hand and he strode confidently towards me stopping just yards short. He lifted the sword threateningly and spoke in that characteristically uncultured voice which contrasted with the fine clothes that he chose to wear.

'My necklace please Citizen.'

Even now I noticed the sarcasm that oozed from his use of this form of address. I reversed the cane that I was carrying and stepped forward with the weighted head raised ready to strike. It quickly became obvious that the bloody fool who had written the pamphlet knew little about self defence as a stride and a slash of the sword left blood pouring down my arm and my only method of defence tumbling down the rock face.

'As I said. My necklace please Citizen or I will be happy to slash your body into a thousand cuts just as I did with your friend Guillot.'

7

I felt faint. The blood was coursing down my arm and I had a sword pointed at my neck. A wrong move now would see me dead for sure. I stalled to try to gain some time. But actually I really wanted to know the answer to my question.

'You were dead?'

I spoke in a gasp whilst holding on to the bridge side. I was not one of these soldiers who fought on with blood pouring from multiple wounds. I was a lawyer who could not even defend himself. I had fled from the Citizen's army in Versailles and now it looked as if I were destined to die here in a foreign land.

De La Motte took another step forward and now the sword was pricking my neck.

* * *

'I would have been if I had not been followed by a companion. When you pushed me into the water I was sorely wounded and would have died within minutes. He chose to pull me out and take me for medical aid rather than apprehending you.

Once you were aboard ship you were out of our reach. However, I knew of your friend's life in Bordeaux and when I was told that it was the next destination of your vessel, once I had recovered, the rest was easy.'

I knew that the necklace would not satisfy his need for revenge. I could give up its whereabouts but he would certainly run me through anyway. I was feeling weaker by the minute and my vision was blurring when a shot rang out. De La Motte crumpled to the ground in front of me and lay still.

I awoke in my own bed with my arm washed and bound. I felt weak but as I pushed myself up, the door opened and in came William Beckford. His face was grim as he sat on a chair at the side of my bed.

'I think that you had better tell me the full story now. It appears that I have just killed a man on your behalf and from what little I could hear of his story on the bridge, it seems that I have done a better job then you did.'

Beckford was a good listener and didn't interrupt as I went back over the affair of the Queen's necklace that De La Motte had instigated. He smiled wryly when he heard how Marie Antoinette had turned the situation to her advantage amidst all of the confusion and secreted the necklace away for herself. He didn't seem surprised when I told him of my friend Guillot and his life as a thief and he appeared to accept calmly when I told him of the current whereabouts of the necklace and that it was now in my ownership.

A few moments after I had finished I discovered the reason for his calm demeanour. He walked to the door, signalled down the corridor and I heard footsteps approaching.

Through the door walked Guillot himself. He was limping and looked pale but the expression on his face showed how delighted he was to see me.

It was a little while before he was ready to tell me his story and it was necessary for him to sit down whilst he did so. In the meantime, Beckford explained how he had come to be near to the bridge with a loaded pistol that morning and had saved my life.

He had been woken by a servant explaining that there was a French gentleman who had just arrived and was desperate to see him urgently. He had dressed quickly and had been confronted by Guillot who had told the same story as the one that I had just related. He was able to add that he had followed De La Motte from Sintra that very morning and that he feared for my safety. Beckford had sprung into action and had charged the weapon and then raced to the bridge where he knew I would be found. Seeing the sword at my throat he had shot De La Motte stone dead.

His servants had been following him and it was they who had carried me back to the house and tended my wound. He had insisted that he talk to me alone to establish that the story that he had been told by Guillot tallied with my own. Satisfied, he had then signalled Guillot to approach and so here we were.

What I didn't know, of course, was Guillot's part in all of this. How had he survived De La Motte's clutches and how did he come to be here. I was soon to find out. It was a grim tale.

He had been going about his business in Bordeaux and in fact had not long left his home when he was walking past an alleyway and was grabbed by a ruffian and pulled into the shadows. He was wrestled to the ground and a cloth sack pulled over his head. A fierce blow to the head ensured that he remained still whilst a second pair of hands bound him. He was bundled into a covered wagon and driven down towards the docks. It turned out that it was a deserted warehouse where he was unloaded like a piece of meat. He was confronted by two men whom he did not recognise. One in particular was finely dressed and it was he that had carried out the interrogation. When he introduced himself as Nicholas De La Motte, Guillot knew that this was not going to go well. Firstly, if this man was who he claimed to be, he had returned from the grave. Secondly, if he had any intention at all of letting my friend go free, he would not have revealed his name.

He was asked one question only - where was I to be found. By this time Guillot had been hung by the wrists from a beam with only his toes touching the ground. His shirt had been cut from his back so he was naked from the waist upwards. At his first refusal to answer the question, De La Motte had pulled out his sword and made a small scratch on Guillot's arm. The second refusal resulted in a scratch on his back. The blood ran down from them and from a third and a fourth and a fifth. This went on for what seemed to be hours until he was weak and delirious. He had been braver than I would have been but inevitably he broke and revealed my address in Lisbon.

The events that followed were uncertain and he had to be told about them later. Upon breaking his man De La Motte spoke to his colleague who had been a passive onlooker during this time. He told him that he was stepping out to the harbour to arrange passage from Bordeaux to Lisbon. At this point Guillot was slipping in and out of consciousness, weakened by the acute loss of blood.

Whether they would have left him to die slowly covered in his own blood or whether they would have finished him off was uncertain, but suddenly voices could be heard, a door opened and a shot rang out. Help had arrived led by his betrothed Susanna. It appeared that the abduction had been seen by a boy in the street who knew him. He had raced to Susanna's house to tell her what had happened and she had raised a well armed body of men to search for me. It appears that it was in her nature to lead the way and after checking the direction in which the cart had travelled they had conducted a search of every empty building and warehouse in that area. De La Motte's colleague was stone dead but they were unable to locate De La Motte himself, presumably having heard the uproar he had made himself scarce. Guillot himself was severely weakened and it was several days before he felt able to travel down the coast to Lisbon to find and warn me. During that time De La Motte had first located and then had followed me. He had overheard the plans that had been made to visit Sintra and had made arrangements to follow. It had obviously been him that I saw climbing into the carriage as I was leaving.

Guillot was in no fit state to travel and I was shaken and

weak. The next days passed in a blur of books and sleep with the evenings being passed as Beckford further showed off his skills on the piano. It turned out that Guillot was no mean musician himself and he took his turn in providing the entertainment. Visitors came and went and Beckford continued his work in the grounds of the estate. He had already constructed the false waterfall and bridge and now was working on a fake medieval folly. He was immensely rich and once I had completed my story, he took no further interest in the Queen's necklace. Likewise, I was sensible enough not to pry further into his exodus from England. The fact that he had saved my life and then disposed of the body showed the man for what he really was.

It was a week later that he introduced us to the owner of a nearby estate which went by the name of Quinta da Torre. If I thought that Beckford was slightly eccentric, this Portuguese gentleman seemed to be from another world. To be more exact, he dressed and acted as though he were of Egyptian origin. Egypt and all things Egyptian were popular amongst the wealthy of Europe but this man had taken it to the extreme. Having said this, he was friendly enough and invited the three of us to visit his home the following day. Both Guillot and myself had recovered sufficiently to make this short trip and in fact, Guillot was talking about returning to Bordeaux within the coming week.

The next day was misty and damp but the three of us took a carriage down towards the town. I had passed the walls of the Quinta da Torre on several occasions and the glimpses that had been afforded showed extensive grounds around a sumptuous palace. We clattered in through the gates and pulled up in front of an exuberantly decorated building. It was constructed of white stone and rose into the sky.

Extravagant carved decorations surrounded the windows and doors and the building was topped with a large turret. It was an impressive place. We were greeted by a manservant who led us through a marble hall into a drawing room that had been decorated in the Italian renaissance style. Our host, the Baron da Regaleira, was stood in front of the window and he turned and greeted us warmly. After we were settled he offered us refreshment and then asked us about the situation in France. The whole of Europe was watching the country closely and the aristocratic families in particular were worried that the troubles might spread further afield. We answered his questions as best we could and after a while he declared that it was time for lunch. The weather was brightening up and he had arranged that a table be laid on the panoramic terrace. It was obvious that he and Beckford were old friends and it was no surprise when he mentioned that he had spent several years in London before coming home to Portugal.

The food was splendid but it was surpassed by the view. I was amazed when we stepped out into the emerging sunshine and looked to see, across the plains that lay below, a vista that took in the distant ocean. We spent the rest of the afternoon in this splendid place and we were questioned further about the situation at home. Why had it happened? How did the Royal Family become so alienated from the people? In return, he told us a little about himself and the Regaleira family. The Quinta was not the original family home but he had bought it after returning to Portugal. From the little that we had seen of it, it was not difficult to see why. He also dropped hints about lavish and extravagant parties that he hosted and after a strange look towards Beckford, offered an invitation to myself and Guillot to attend one the following week. Beckford himself was obviously a regular guest at these events and other than a nod of the head in reply to the look from da Regaleira, said nothing. Guillot declined the invitation, simply explaining that he needed to return to Bordeaux as quickly as possible. I though was intrigued and accepted immediately. I was a little concerned about the appropriate dress for an occasion such as this but Beckford allayed my fears by saying that it would be a costume event and that he had a wide range of suitable garments, some of which were bound to fit me. I asked for more information but they would give nothing away, simply saying that surprise was a key element.

The week passed quickly spent largely perusing a strange book that was given to me by Beckford. It was titled Crata Repoa and was written in Latin, a language that I knew because of my background as a lawyer. It spoke of ancient rituals and rites of initiation and seemed to have a myriad of authors. Frequent reference was made to Ancient Egypt and its gods and kings and although I consider myself to be a reasonably scholarly man, I have to say that I could make no real sense of the fragments that made up the text. Guillot departed during that week and we made a solemn promise to stay in touch. He wanted me to meet Susanna and I was particularly intrigued to find what it was that had converted a man of adventure into a respectable citizen.

I too felt that it was my turn to depart returning first to Lisbon and then perhaps to Porto. Beckford had been extremely generous as a host but I could not stay here forever. However, the mysterious party loomed and I had become extremely intrigued by some of Beckford's asides. Several times he had started to comment but had stopped himself before saying anything of any worth. All that I could get from him was that it would be a party like no other and that I should leave behind all of my preconceptions.

The morning arrived and I took my customary stroll to the waterfall and the bridge. I had only been enjoying the tranquility for a few minutes when Beckford appeared, this time in less of a hurry and walking along the track rather than rushing through the trees. He greeted me cordially and then immediately started to talk about the day's events. When we were ready to start our preparations I was to bathe and then don the robes that he had prepared for me. I was told to expect the unusual and again to approach the gathering with an open mind. I was to take the Crata Repoa with me as it would play an important part in the proceedings. It sounded like a most peculiar party but I was reluctant to question him further. He had been an exemplary host and somewhat more importantly to me, he had saved my life. I trusted him and I trusted his judgement. It was obviously going to be an evening that I would remember for a long time but when I made this comment to him, he gave me a strange glance and nodded sombrely.

'I can guarantee that will be the case.'

We returned to the house together and he took great delight in pointing out some of the exotic looking flowers that he insisted would not be seen in northern Europe.

After we had eaten an extensive breakfast, I went to my room to continue reading. It was much later in the day when a servant arrived to prepare a bath which steamed and smelled of exotic oils. I took my time soaking but eventually the water had cooled to a point where it was necessary to retreat. On my bed, robes had been laid out which resembled those that I seen on the Baron da Regaleira a week earlier. The craze for all things Egyptian which was popular in Europe made them instantly recognisable as a copy of the formal clothing of an Egyptian pharaoh. They were patterned with gold thread and a silver design embellished the chest. It was an image of an eye with rays of light shining through it. I did not recognise it but I was certain that I would learn more of its significance later in the day. A fez, also in gold, completed the ensemble. It felt strange at first although I could see the practicality of the outfit in a country with such hot weather.

I picked up the book that I had been requested to bring and made my way to the drawing room downstairs to find Beckford clad in an equally bizarre fashion.

'And don't we look a pair', he laughed as I entered. 'The Baron always insists on this regalia and as the host of this event we are beholden to comply.'

I noticed his use of the word 'event' whereas he had previously been referring to a party and my curiosity was piqued even more.

The carriage was waiting outside the main entrance and as soon as we had climbed in the blinds were pulled across the windows and we set off. This was odd, not least because of the stifling heat, but as I looked quizzically at Beckford he nodded reassuringly and simply said, 'It's necessary. You will understand soon.'

It was apparent that we were travelling downhill and it seemed that no time had passed before we slowed and turned into what I presumed was the entrance. This Palace was just inside the gate although the carriage didn't stop but continued onto a much rougher road travelling this time uphill. We were shaken about somewhat until after ten or so minutes in this fashion, we came to a stop. We had obviously arrived at our destination.

The carriage door was opened from the outside and the last rays of the setting sun streamed in through the trees. It was a strange sight that met my eyes. We had been deposited high up in the grounds of the Palace and a path led away from the carriage up to a balcony, that appeared from here to contain a waist high stone wall with an opening in it. Lanterns had been lit that were obviously intended to illuminate the way after the sun had disappeared. I could hear music - a strange litany that seemed to originate from the balcony itself. We stepped down onto the path and Beckford glanced in my direction saying 'Ready?' I nodded and he stepped past me leading the way. The music grew louder until we reached the balcony itself and I could see that the wall actually surrounded a well. No, in fact not a well, but more like an inverted tower which corkscrewed down into the ground. Now that I was closer I could see a staircase spiralling down around the edge and in the distance at the bottom, set into the tiles, a logo that resembled that on our robes. I could count nine platforms on the staircase and the voices that were chanting were coming from a tunnel that led away from the last step.

Beckford turned towards me looking more solemn than I had ever seen him and said,

'Welcome to the Initiation Well.'

What had I let myself in for?

8

My first reaction was to turn and retreat back to the carriage but I had not noticed three large gentleman clad in black who had followed us up the path. Beckford noticed my alarm and said in a reassuring voicc,

'Trust me. This is a special occasion and I would not allow any harm to befall you. I want you to see what is below and then you can make up your own mind whether to stay or to return.'

He stepped to one side and indicated that I should lead the way down the spiral steps. I had the impression that the characters behind me were intended to prevent any hasty retreat but I must confess that my curiosity was getting the better of me. The stairs were dank and by the time that I reached the first level, the humidity in the air was palpable. It was as I stepped onto the sixth level down I could feel water dripping onto the fez that I wore and down the walls themselves. At the bottom of the Initiation Well I paused to let the others catch up. The music was now echoing around me, emanating seemingly from all three tunnels that led away from the tiled floor. Beckford gestured towards the tunnel on the left and I turned into it, glad to get away from the dripping water. After a short distance the tunnel opened out into a chamber and standing to one side was the Baron da Regaleira himself. He was effusive in his greeting of Beckford and then he turned to me.

'Welcome my friend. Before you progress any further, I would like to offer you an explanation of what you are about to see. If you are unwilling to progress any further then you will be escorted back to your carriage and hence back to Monserrate. The only thing that I ask in return is your word as a gentleman that you will not repeat anything that I am about to divulge.'

   I could not reject this offer and so I replied simply,

'I swear.'

And so the tale began.

It had started in London some eighty years before when a prominent politician by the name of Sir Francis Dashwood formed a gentleman's club with the motto 'Fais ce que tu voudras' which translates into English as 'Do What Thou Wilt'. He had been made a Duke by King George and since that moment had taken it upon himself to live this maxim to its limit. What started as a drinking club descended into a blasphemous, licentious group of wealthy politicians who seemed to be determined to shock civilised England. The members came to the meetings dressed, mockingly, as characters from the bible. They held black masses and worshipped the devil. 'Female guests' dressed as nuns participated in licentious behaviour. The club was eventually closed by Royal edict because of the so called 'corruption of minds and morals'.

The Baron paused to gauge my reaction and asked if I wanted to hear more. Of course I could not let it stop there and so nodded my consent. Beckford took up the tale.

After the cessation of the so called 'Hellfire Club' as it had come to be known, Dashwood initiated other clubs and although eccentric in nature, they were much less contentious. One such club required its members to dress in Turkish robes, another in Roman togas.

The Hellfire Club however had not ceased to exist - it had simply gone underground in order to avoid the King's gaze. It multiplied and held its meetings in various locations. One branch had become associated with ancient Egypt and the clothes that were worn were those of the Pharaohs. The orgies that occurred were with women brought in dressed in slaves clothing. They initiated new members with passages from a book that I had become familiar with - the Crata Repoa. I guessed that the two gentlemen before me had become members whilst in London and this is where they had actually met. It was no coincidence then that they were both here in Sintra having fled from the approbation that came their way when the club had been uncovered two years ago. What I had been invited to attend was an initiation ceremony for their version of the Hellfire Club. What I had to decide was whether I wished to participate in their debauched, blasphemous lifestyle. I had no emotional attachments and as such, could live my life in any way that I chose. I had however, been brought up in a strong Catholic faith and been taught to respect the rights of others. This is why I became a lawyer in the first instance. I could not turn my back on the beliefs that had been ingrained in me and so with a strange feeling of regret and of what I might be missing I declined to step any further.

It goes without saying that they were disappointed in the extreme. They thought that they had seen some common spark in me but they were true to their word and I was escorted back up to the surface and allowed to return in peace to Monserrate. The journey back was tinged with regret, after all, I had turned down the opportunity to participate in what would be most men's dreams. However, my decision was the right one and I was correct in choosing this path.

I made my decision to return to Lisbon the following day. I did not want Beckford trying to change my mind and so that evening I packed my chest and made arrangements for one of the coachman to be ready first thing. I was not sure what time Beckford would return but it was certain that it would not be early. When I had prepared as much as I possibly could for the following day, I retired to the drawing room and poured myself a large Cognac from the cut glass decanter that sat on the large table. I sipped slowly as I considered the events that had taken place during the evening. Many men would not have shown the same restraint that I had but I certainly had no regrets about my decision to leave early. It was with some astonishment then that just minutes later I heard the sound of a horse and carriage sweeping into the drive. The sound of a front door slamming could be heard followed by a voice that was clearly Beckford's. Moments later the man himself swept into the room and pouring a drink for himself sat himself down opposite me.

'My dear chap. Congratulations. You passed the test. By the way, I have told my staff that you will be staying for a few days longer. I hope you don't mind me contradicting your instructions but after what I saw tonight I'm confident that you will wish to stay also.'

All of this came out in somewhat of a rush and as he paused for breath I interrupted, looking at him with what I imagined to be a considerable scowl on my face.

'I do not pass judgement on your preference for the debauchery that I saw tonight but I certainly have no wish to be involved and I cannot possibly imagine how I could have passed any kind of test.'

He had now gathered his breath and surprised me yet again.

'Tonight's test was to see if you would be able to reject the temptations that the Hellfire club would offer you. Most men would have accepted what was on offer but not you my friend. You are cut from a different cloth altogether. No - the test that you passed was altogether contrary. I would in fact like to talk to you about an organisation that I represent which is known as the Brotherhood of the Rosicrucians. The test that you passed was the rejection of the Hellfire Club which shows me that you are worthy of admittance to our order if you so wish. The idea for the initiation test was that of one of our members, a composer of music who built a similar idea into one of his operas.'

'I watched a performance of 'The Magic Flute' in Paris last year. Is that the one of which you speak?'

* * *

'I mention it simply to show that our membership is spread far and wide. Luminaries such as Mr. Newton the English scientist and Mr. Fourier, the mathematician from Paris are amongst our members. Our raison d'être is a charitable one, to aid the poor and the suffering wherever possible but to do it without drawing attention to ourselves. In order to invite a new member, they have to pass a test of one kind or another first. You passed the test of licentiousness and lust. I am now allowed to propose you for membership of our order if you so wish it. You will be joining some of the greatest people of European history.'

'But why me? I am not particularly rich or famous. I can probably contribute little to your cause. I do know Joseph Fourier but as far as he is aware there is little to commend me. I was actually appointed by Robespierre to prosecute him.'

What Fourier did not know, I thought, was that I had actually worked furiously on his behalf and at the time I left Versailles I was fairly certain that his release was imminent.

'You are wrong. Mr. Fourier is well aware of what you have done for him and from news that I heard this evening I do believe that your efforts have been rewarded and that he has been released. I have also heard reports of the dozens if not hundreds of others that you have secretly helped to escape the bloodletting that swamps Paris these days. This is why you have been chosen. We need people who are selfless and have a good heart. It was convenient that the idiot this evening tries to emulate the lunatics from London with his version of the Hellfire club. He tries and tries to invite me and I have always refused. Tonight however was a perfect opportunity to test your resolve.'

I was puzzled.

'But what if I was not so inclined. What then?'

'As I said, we have a number of possible tests. Mr. Mozart is fond of initiations by fire and water but I prefer to see a solid heart and spirit as you have shown. You are worthy of a place amongst us.'

To say that I was stunned would be an understatement. I had tried to keep my activities in Paris as secretive as possible but it did explain why I was being hunted by the Committee. It seems that I fled in the nick of time but without realising the true nature of my accusers. But what of De La Motte? Was it just greed or was there something more? I could not keep up with the whirl of thoughts that were spinning round in my head so, with my greatest apologies, I bid Beckford good night and promised him an answer in the morning. After the events of the day my sleep was fitful and as the birds began their pre-dawn chorus and the world changed from black to a dark shade of grey I had still not decided whether to take the man up on his offer. Paris was still too dangerous a place for me but my money was running out at a great rate. I could not practise my trade in the law here in Portugal without a more thorough knowledge of the language and a number of years intense study. I believed that France was changing and that the Reign of Terror was coming to an end but it would be some time before I could go back and continue with my life. I had a decision to make and in all honesty, there was only one choice for a man in my position.

It's a strange thing at dawn that the scenery goes from a

range of blacks and greys into a vivid multi-coloured panorama in just a few minutes. I had let myself out of the house and was walking towards the bridge where I had faced De La Motte just a few days ago. I was looking back towards the house when the rising sun turned the world from a monochromatic landscape into one that made the heart sing. I knew now what I had to do. When I returned to the house Beckford was waiting. He obviously had a vested interest in my answer although for the life of me I couldn't see why. I wasn't ready yet to agree to join his organisation without knowing much more about my commitment although truth be told, I had few choices left to me.

'We are certain that France will return to some sort of normality within a year or two and it would be to our benefit if we had a powerful lawyer in Paris who could intervene on occasion in worthy cases. In return we are more than happy to financially support you until you are able to go back. If you so wish, it would not be necessary to attend any of our meetings although you may well find them both instructive and educational. We encourage our members whether they be scientist, artist or musician to break their travels throughout Europe by providing a place for them to stay in return for their insights into their world.'

And so I joined the Order of the Rosicrucians albeit I was not able to offer any kind of immediate contribution to their worthy cause. I stayed with Beckford for another week and it was fortunate that I did so because it was then that I received an update from my dear friend Guillot. He had arrived back in Bordeaux without incident and was now almost fully recovered from his ordeal, a few scars apart that is. He had resumed his trading business and begged me to let him know when I returned to Porto so that he could instigate another visit.

I had become great friends with Beckford and so it was with some regret that I said goodbye with a promise to return soon. Hearing from Guillot had decided me that I wanted to spend time in Porto perhaps breaking into the wine trade that was so dominated by the English. It appeared that I now had powerful contacts and so it should be possible to make inroads. It seemed a bizarre idea but the fortified wine of Porto was very different to those wines produced in France and a close friend of mine was now in the import export business in Bordeaux with ships travelling between the two cities. I was looking forward to the challenge.

The next two years passed quickly. I was able to purchase my rented house in Porto at a very reasonable rate and with Beckford's contacts in the City Hall smoothing my path, I was quickly buying Porto wine in quantity and using Guillot's ships to send it to the main wine centre in France. Much to my surprise it was popular with the wealthy French middle class and it sold out there at a quicker rate than I was able to buy it.

Everything was looking good when news started to filter through of the demise of the Revolutionary Council and news of a certain General Bonaparte who had come from nowhere to take on the leadership of my country. It would be several years later that he would designate himself Emperor and set Europe aflame but at this stage he was being seen as something of a saviour, restoring normality to France and even winning military battles against old enemies.

I decided that the time had come to see the French side of my business venture and so installing a trustworthy manager in place, I locked up my house and boarded one of Guillot's clippers to head for Bordeaux. It was now several years since I had left my country of birth and in some ways Bordeaux was as different to me as had been Porto and Lisbon when I first arrived. That changed quickly however, as with my friends help I found somewhere to live and took over the running of this end of my business. Time passed quickly and news from Paris arrived more frequently than it had been able to reach Portugal. My old enemies were being disgraced and the situation was almost now back to normal - except that is for one massive change. We were no longer ruled by the Royal Family and the influence of the aristocracy had been massively diminished. The rule of law was everything and so the time arrived when I could make plans to return to Versailles and resume my career.

My return home was greeted with great joy and happiness by my family. They hadn't understood the need for me to flee the country but accepted that it was important to me. I had been able to let them know that I was alive and well but I daren't give out much more information than that for fear of their torture. My house had been well cared for and I was able to move back in immediately. My law practise in Paris resumed smoothly and I quickly regained many of my old clients. After all of my adventures my old life was slipping back into place exactly as it had been, except of course, for the fact that I knew that I had a debt to pay. Oh yes - and there was the small matter of the Queen's necklace. It had caused so much trouble and so many deaths I was uncertain as to the best thing to do with it. And so it stayed in its resting place, wrapped in a blue velvet bag, concealed in the wall cavity up in the attic space.

9

The house was large and imposing. Built on the cliff top with an old smugglers path between the garden wall and the cliff itself, it dominated the view. I sat on a rock admiring the contrast between the red gate and shutters and the brilliant blue of the sky. When I turned and looked in the opposite direction the sea sparkled with points of light and white fishing boats danced on the waves. It was a bittersweet moment but the overwhelming feeling of sadness soon returned.

It seemed that I was destined to lose someone close to me whilst inheriting treasures that I hadn't asked for.

My name is Paul Breslin and I am a history detective. OK, it does sound a little pretentious but my publishers insist on using it for my biographical info and to be honest I actually quite like it. So it stays. Twelve months ago my friend and mentor, William Scott, died under tragic circumstances. He left me a fortune, a Chateau in the Loire Valley and indirectly my business manager Gaston Lestrade. Gaston and I have a healthy arrangement. He does what it says on the tin and manages my business portfolio for me. That leaves me free to do what I am good at. Detecting history.

It just takes the sniff of an old dusty manuscript to set me off and even excluding the events that took place whilst William was alive, I have tracked down two missing paintings and one first edition in the last twelve months. Of course, there have also been numerous blind alleys and wild goose chases as well but that made the end results even better. Apart from the immense feeling of satisfaction that it gives, I have netted several hundred thousand pounds in the process. Gaston, of course, likes to point out that my businesses, that he manages, have brought in several million euros in the same period. Less his commission of course. I have only known him for a year but he was trusted implicitly by William and he is earning a lot of money by making money for me. And yes - I realise that I still think in sterling whenever possible despite living in France but I am sure that if Gaston had the chance, he would do the same. French by birth, an eccentric anglophile by choice.

So naturally I was surprised when he went missing. I use the word loosely as he did ask for leave of absence whilst I attended my grandmother's funeral here in Brittany but he left no contact details and now I haven't heard from him for a number of days. It's not a problem yet but it is extremely unusual. No - scratch that. It's the first time since we met that I haven't been able to get a fairly immediate response either by mobile phone or email.

* * *

Soon I would have to make a decision. I had lived for the previous year in the Chateau in the Loire Valley that William had passed on to me. However, I had spent most of my summer holidays as a child here in Locquirec and I had happy, fond memories of the rambling old building. It was always a sad moment when the new school term was starting and I had to return to my home in England. Conversely, the tower in the Chateau from which William had fallen to his death seemed cold and austere - a place to be tolerated not loved. I knew that I had already made a decision but the complications of the move had to be overcome. I suspected that Gaston would want to remain in situ. He had worked for many years for William Scott before I had arrived and although he had agreed to continue to manage the business side of things for me, his heart was firmly entrenched where it was. It was also much easier for Gaston to travel to Paris and Versailles where he had property. I would also need to talk to Guilbert and Patrice, nominally the gardener and cook who had stayed on after William's demise. However, for the moment, there was an obligation to return inside and make polite conversation with those who had attended the funeral.

The next morning, I was woken by the bright sunlight reflecting off the sea and in through the bedroom window. I slipped out of bed without disturbing the figure next to me. Whilst most of the mourners had been elderly friends of my grandmother, I had been delighted to see that a childhood friend of mine had arrived from Paris to pay her respects. Alicia had been brought up in the little fishing port of Locquirec then after leaving University had moved to Paris to work for a prestigious law firm. She and I were occasional lovers and she had taken no persuading to spend the night with me before returning to the capital. I dressed quietly and went to rediscover the old house. It was only a letter that I had received earlier in the year from the old lady that had alerted me to the fact that I was her only surviving relative and that the house would eventually pass into my possession. However, until I received confirmation from the notaire that was dealing with the will, nothing was final. I had already decided that if it was passed to someone else I was going to buy it back - no matter the cost. One room in particular caught my fancy - up on the third floor with a large picture window - it would make a superb study for my research - assuming that the amazing view didn't constantly interrupt my work.

As I said, one of the advantages of employing Gaston to manage the multiple businesses was that it released time for me to pursue my work as a historian. I had published several books which had been well received but following my adventures last year and my new financial independence I really was starting to think that the publishers flannel about the history detective might actually be me. Guessing that internet broadband would not be great out here on the cliffs, I made a mental note to investigate satellite internet connection. The internet, my antique desk and access to my music were all that I needed to work. Gaston was still worrying me and it was important that I speak to him today but the dapper Frenchman was still not answering his mobile phone or replying to my emails. It was irritating but still not a real concern as he was taking his first real break in over a year and I was guessing that he had switched off in all possible ways.

A creak on the staircase made me turn to see Alicia, wrapped in a bed sheet, standing on the landing. I had always teased her about her prudishness but she simply laughed and then ignored me. Hoping that she was going to suggest returning to bed I moved towards her just as she grinned, lifted a finger and mouthed 'No! I have a train to catch and you need to run me to the station.'

'I'm gutted but I'll let you off this time. Anyway, you wore me out last night.'

Again she smiled and replied. 'Liar, but I do need to get back to work as soon as possible. It's an important case that we are working on and they were not really happy to let me go to the funeral of an old friend. I told them that I was going anyway and that they would have to manage without me for two days. If I get the train later this morning, I can be back in the office for this afternoon.'

'OK. Shower, quick breakfast and we can be away in under an hour. Half an hour to the TGV station and you will have disappeared from my life again.'

I dropped Alicia with time to spare at Guingamp station with promises of a visit to Paris soon. The drive back through the pretty Breton countryside seemed to take no time at all and I soon found myself re-entering the tall granite house that I had decided was to become my new home. It was very quiet inside and very old fashioned. Climbing the stairs to the top floor again I sat down at the old dark wooden table that was placed in front of the window and pulled out my MacBook. Despite the fact that the old lady had not seen the need for an internet connection, even if one was available in this remote place, I had a trick that my friend Andres from Granada had shown me. It was a matter of a few moments to set up my mobile phone as a wifi router and soon my laptop was connecting to my email account. Time to try to contact

Gaston again. Having sent yet another email, it was then necessary to deal with the myriad of messages in my inbox. The rest of the morning flew past quickly.

Versailles in spring is a beautiful town. The buildings look clean and smart and the boulevard leading to the Chateau is full of trees. Gaston Lestrade however, was oblivious to all of this. The apartment in which he was impatiently waiting had belonged to his family for a number of centuries and in fact it was said that the Lestrade's had once owned all of the house. Now it consisted of three beautiful apartments, each covering an entire floor, with the Lestrade residence taking prime spot at the very top. It was unoccupied for much of the time as Gaston himself lived and worked in the Loire Valley, first for the late William Scott, 14th Earl of Strathearn and now as business manager for Paul Breslin. His younger sister Lillian lived and worked in Paris although Gaston was unclear about what she actually did. He had been surprised when a week earlier she had contacted him by email begging him to come to the apartment and wait for her. It was critically important she said, that no one knew where he was and that he might have to wait patiently for her to arrive. She was in desperate trouble and needed his help. This in itself was something of a shock as Lillian was fiercely independent - in fact almost bordering on anarchistic. Gaston had seen little of her in the last three years but recognised that a plea such as the one that he had received must mean that something was seriously wrong. It was annoying and irritating that he had been asked to wait for an indeterminate amount of time but when he had replied to her email his message had been bounced back with a tag stating *'email address unknown'*.

She had obviously used a temporary proxy of some kind -

but why?

He had been here for three days with no indication when Lillian might arrive, scarcely daring to go out in case he missed her. It was pointless speculating about the kind of trouble that she might be in but suffice it to say that it must be extremely serious. He had received no further communication from her. His email box was filling up rapidly but he dare not start replying to them. Her instructions had been very precise. No one must know where he was and no communication of any kind once he had arrived. The room in which he spent most of his time was lined with bookshelves, each filled with books that had been collected by the family over the centuries of habitation here. Some of the leather bound volumes dated back to the 18th century. He had pulled out a number of them and idly flicked through the pages to kill the time whilst he waited but he did find the archaic language very tedious and most had been quickly returned. One tome however, had captured his interest. It was a journal - handwritten by one of his ancestors dated back to the 1780's. It described his life as a lawyer in pre-revolutionary Paris. Frustratingly, it ended with a brief reference to a plan to purchase a new property in Versailles.

Presumably, thought Gaston, *the same building in which I'm now waiting.*

The sun was streaming in through the large windows and Gaston was sat with the journal in front of him when he was startled by a voice.

'Greetings dear brother. I see that you still affect the English mode of dress. I thought that you would have realised by now that it is really a caricature.'

Stepping into the room, Lillian walked across to him and held out her arms. Gaston stood and awkwardly embraced her. It was a very long time since they had shown any real affection towards one another.

'Thank you for coming. Until I saw your coat in the hallway I was unsure if you would be here. Have you done as I asked? No-one must know of your whereabouts.'

'I have done exactly as you asked at, I must say, a great deal of inconvenience to a number of people. I assume that the trouble that you're in is pretty desperate. Tell me everything.'

Lillian sat down opposite her brother and looked at him for several seconds while she decided where to start. From her appearance, it would be impossible to guess that these two had been brought up in the same family. Where Gaston dressed in what he described as the 'English style' of tweed and brogues, Lillian looked like a punk who had time travelled from the seventies. Her black jeans were ripped in a number of places, her dyed black hair spiked and gelled and piercings in her bottom lip and nose completed the illusion. It had been difficult for her to ask for help from her older brother and now she was unsure how to start.

'Go back to the beginning,' prompted Gaston. 'It's two years since I saw you last. If I'm going to help, I need to know everything.'

Slowly at first then with increasing confidence, Lillian told her tale.

* * *

'As you know, I left home under something of a cloud. I was thrown out of school and mum and dad were less than impressed. This was when you were working for the English Lord.'

'He was Scottish, he was an Earl and he died last year.' growled Gaston. Now continue.'

'OK. Sorry. Well I couldn't stay here with that atmosphere so I left for Paris. I had no job to go to and few prospects of getting one. However, I did have a friend who had a few rooms in the Pigalle district and she let me stay. What you don't know is that I was thrown out of school for hacking the school network in order to change my grades.'

Gaston interrupted again. 'But your grades were excellent. I remember that everyone was convinced that you had a promising future ahead of you.'

For the first time since entering the room, Lillian smiled and chortled 'No. I had got in with a crowd who despised good grades. I was hacking to reduce them. I still don't know how they caught me. Anyway, I was good at maths and I was brilliant with computers. In Paris though, nobody wanted to employ someone who had been expelled from school just weeks from the end of the last term. I needed money so when my friend introduced me to this man, I was happy to take any work that he offered.'

'Please don't tell me that you went on the street.'

Again, Lillian giggled. 'You are such an old fashioned prude. What if I did?'

* * *

She waited for a moment and then continued.

'No I didn't. He offered me a job working with computers. He'd been told about my genius and he offered me enough money to live comfortably provided that I passed a test that he had lined up. Of course I jumped at the chance. The day after I was introduced to him I went to an office near to Les Halles. He was there with two other men and they asked me to demonstrate my hacking skills. It was simplicity itself to get back into the school system. The idiots hadn't even found the trapdoor that I had left. I made some changes and it seemed to impress them enough to start asking me about writing code. They asked me to write programs to carry out what seemed to be trivial meaningless tasks so I obliged. It was simple enough. I started work there the following day. At first it was writing simple apps and games that were sold online for a few euros. After a few weeks they asked if I minded adding a few lines that created pop up adverts on the client's computer. It's mildly illegal but I wasn't going to lose a good job over that. Anyway, most people have got anti malware software running and if they haven't they deserve all they get. After that all of the apps that we released contained malware. It was no big deal.'

She sensed that Gaston was about to interrupt but stopped him saying, 'No. That's not what caused the bother. It got worse. They let this run for a few more months and I was getting paid well. That's when it escalated. They then asked me if I could create some malware that would invisibly log the keystrokes on a computer and upload a file of the results to an anonymous server. I could see where this was going. It would be an easy way of collecting login details from anyone who was banking online. At first I refused. I was OK with the low level stuff but this was guaranteed prison for anyone who was caught. That's when they told me that they would compromise me for what I had been doing on their behalf during the last few months. They had put together a file that would be sent to the police which contained enough evidence to prove that I was responsible for programs that I hadn't created. At that point, I realised that I was stuffed. I really had no choice but to go along with them.

Gaston frowned before commenting, 'There's always a choice. You just have to make the right one.'

'Yeah right. Like I had a choice. Carry on earning shedloads of money or jail time. Anyway, this carried on for a few more months. By now, I had my own apartment which they loaned me the money to buy. No pressure over repayments either. I thought that I'd made the right decision.'

'But then it escalated again' interrupted Gaston.

For the first time Lillian looked abashed.

' You always were too clever by half. Private individuals were obviously small fry. When they demanded that I target financial organisations I realised that I was in way over my head. This time, I told them what they could do with their job and their loan but they took it kind of personally. I told them that if they grassed me to the police I would take them down with me. So they introduced me to the Mouse. God alone knows where he got the name from. He was scary. He described in detail the kind of things that they did to anyone who upset them. He was so quiet but obviously relished what he did. And then they told me that they knew about you and where you were living. You remember the last email that you sent. Stupidly, I had talked about my older brother and his work for the Englishman. They had followed it up and the threats weren't just aimed at me. They promised to get you first and make me watch.

10

At last, Gaston saw the enormity of the problem facing his young sister. He was not particularly worried about the threats against himself but it was obvious that she was in grave danger. As he mused over what she had just told him she dropped another bombshell.

'When I left Paris I thought that I had escaped undetected, but as I got off the metro here I saw a man that I recognised at the other end of the platform. He'd been in and out of the office on odd occasions, obviously working for them and I think that he saw me. When I left the subway I tried to make sure that he wasn't following me. I went through several department stores checking in the mirrors all the time. I don't think that he saw me come here but they are probably scouring the town.'

* * *

'In that case we need to get out. I have some friends who can help us but I will have to tell them what you have told me. They will be discrete and they are much better equipped to deal with this situation than we are.'

Lillian's protests were brushed aside. 'It's too late for secrecy. You need all the help that you can get.'

Gaston pulled out his mobile phone and winced at the scrolling list of missed calls and notifications of unanswered emails and text messages. Both Guilbert and Patrice were on speed dial for him. They had been employed by the late William Scott at about the same time that he had started but unlike Gaston these men were used to violence. They had both been employed by an obscure branch of the French Secret Service and when it was shut down they both decided to retire. It was a mystery how William Scott had heard about them and even more of a mystery how he persuaded them to work nominally as his gardener and chef. However, as Gaston himself had witnessed last year, they had lost none of their skills and he was confident that they could easily deal with these criminals. The trouble was neither of them answered his call. It wasn't surprising really as Paul Breslin had agreed that they could all take a break whilst he attended the funeral of his grandmother in Brittany. This had suited Gaston perfectly but it was obvious that Paul now needed him and he had been coerced into maintaining secrecy as to his whereabouts. Now, it was likely that Guilbert and Patrice were taking advantage of the cheap wine that would be flowing for the celebrations of Bastille Day - the biggest holiday in France. There would be time to contact Paul with apologies and explanations later but he was not the one who could help in the immediate crisis. He had to get his sister back to the chateau and to the protection of his friends.

'We are going to have to do this ourselves. My car is parked in the underground car park on level -3. It's the green Jaguar. We are going to make our way there and drive to Le Château de la Croix which is on the outskirts of a village called Montignac between Blois and Amboise.'

Even now, almost a year after William's untimely death, Gaston found it difficult to think of the property as Paul's even though his new employer had been exceedingly generous. It did have the advantage of being some distance from Paris though and once there help would be at hand.

The apartment was immaculate and all he had to do was place the journal back on the shelf and he was ready to go. Gaston pulled the curtain to one side and looked out of the window to the street below. There were people going about their business but he could see no one that looked as though they were watching the apartment. He took his tweed jacket from the rack in the hallway, put it on, briefly checked his appearance in the mirror then opened the door. He was relieved to see no one on the landing so locking the door carefully he set off down the wide oak staircase with Lillian following close behind. At the bottom he stopped and spoke a few words to the concierge. No, there had been no one asking questions about them and no strangers lurking about either. Carefully stepping out into the street, he looked around. Still clear so he led the way down to the main road and round the corner towards the car park entrance. Suddenly Lillian pulled on his arm.

'Over there, that's one of them.'

Gaston groaned inwardly. At that same moment it was obvious that they had been seen and the man was between them and the car park. They couldn't go back to the apartment without being followed there so he turned and crossed the road. Directly opposite was a street that ran parallel to the Palace. It was cobbled and led towards the public park that skirted the Palace grounds. They started to run and at the end turned sharply left through the large gates. A long way behind them a second man had joined the first. Parkland stretched out in front of them with paths going in all directions.

Thinking quickly Gaston ran to the left towards a cubical that marked one of many entrances into the Versailles Palace gardens. Pulling out a handful of notes he dropped them on the counter and carried on running without collecting their tickets. If they could lose them in the acres ahead there were too many exits for the two men to cover. Emerging between two rows of beech hedges they came out onto the grand canal. Looking up, Gaston was startled to see an impossible giant waterfall apparently dropping out of the sky. It took a moment before he remembered that he had read about this water feature being installed since he had last visited. Without pausing he ran past the structure and towards the 'bosquets' a series of grottos that almost formed a labyrinth. If they could reach them first, there was every chance that they could escape undetected.

He sensed Lillian running just behind him but it was becoming harder and harder to catch his breath. He looked back to see the two men following some two hundred metres behind them. The tall hedge of the perimeter of the first bosquet was just in front of them now so he turned, grabbed Lillian's arm and dragged her inside. It was like stepping into another world. In the centre was a large lake containing several fountains. Incongruously the fountains were pulsing and shooting water spouts high into the sky, baroque music played through hidden speakers and several dozen people watched entranced by the show. Without stopping they forced their way through the crowded area provoking grunts of protest from the spectators. Once out of the other side they emerged from this first grotto and with a choice of three more entrances in front of them, Gaston chose the bosquet immediately to their right for no better reason than it was marginally the nearest. This time the water show had finished and the crowd had already dispersed. Out of the far side and another random choice. Again, a grotto with more fountains and more music. At last he stopped to let them catch their breath. He doubted that the criminals would have been lucky enough to blindly choose the two paths that they had made at random but just to be sure he urged Lillian onwards once more and they made their way through two more of the glades at random. Because each was surrounded by high hedges and had multiple exits, it was impossible to see who was inside each one without actually entering it.

Stopping again to catch his breath Gaston took the opportunity to look around. They were now just a fast five minute walk away from the main terrace that was at the rear of the Versailles Palace. The problem was that most of the distance was covered with open lawns and paths with very little cover. If the pursuers happened to turn this way they could not avoid being seen. Thinking quickly Gaston scanned the ground around him and instructed Lillian to wait within the relative safety of the hedged area that they were in. To his surprise she agreed without any argument at all, an obvious indication of how scared she really was.

Trying to hide the concern that he felt he smiled in her direction and stepped out into the open ground. Constantly checking over his shoulder he was about half way across when he realised that he had been seen. They had emerged from one of the hedged grottos that was some distance to the right of where he had left his sister. She, at least, was safe for the moment. He could see the dilemma that he had set them though. First of all he was alone so did they both follow him and increase their probability of catching him, continue to search the grottoes for Lillian or split up and thereby improve the odds in his favour. The moments that they took to make a decision allowed him to get closer to the broad elegant steps leading up towards the building and he was relieved when they both decided to stay in pursuit of him. As they increased their pace he carefully judged his own so that they were within a hundred metres or so when he reached the top. Still there, to his relief, were two armed gendarmes that he had noticed when he had set off.

They had been out of sight from the steps but they were carefully scanning the crowd and had noticed his hurried approach. By now he was out of line of sight of the men below and it only took a few moments for him to gasp about men with guns and describe them to the officers. With so much terrorist activity in France and particularly in Paris he didn't need to add anything further before they had pulled out their weapons and approached the top of the steps. Sure enough the two that he had described were three quarters of the way up and the surprised expression on their faces when they saw two gendarmes pointing their weapons at them made Gaston smile even under these circumstances. They were forced to the ground, handcuffed and searched. Gaston was relieved to see that both had guns concealed underneath their jackets. It had been a bit of a gamble but it had paid off. He could see Lillian in the distance so he waved her forward and waited for her while the area was cleared by the extra police that had been radioed in. He declined to leave his name simply saying that one of the men had allowed his jacket to swing open and he had seen what appeared to be a gun. Before they could insist he slipped away into the crowd that the gendarmes were trying to move away and edged around until he could see his sister. Joining up they made their way towards the exit.

Thirty minutes later they were sat in Gaston's racing green Jaguar saloon. 'Another English affectation?' queried Lillian with a smirk. For the first time since she had slipped into the apartment however, Gaston suspected that there was an element of bravado about her comments, a method of keeping face when in fact, she had just been through the most terrifying morning of her life. He ignored her and concentrated on negotiating the traffic whilst trying to make telephone contact using the bluetooth system built into the car, first of all with Guilbert and then with Patrice. Neither were responding. 'Too much red wine' he growled. 'Bloody Bastille Day.'

'So why not contact your Patron?'

'I really don't want to involve him in my problems if possible. These two are always ready for a fight - it's what they did for a living for many years but Paul is an academic - a historian. It was purely by accident that he got caught up in the mess last year which saw him inherit the late Earl's business interests. He is a nice man but I can't see how he can help under these circumstances. Guilbert and Patrice are the ones that can help us to sort this out and if they can't they will certainly have contacts that can. However, I need to know more about this mess. Think hard. What have you told them about me and about my friends. What do they actually know?'

Lillian closed her eyes and savoured the smell of leather that permeated the car. For a moment she thought that she could forget all about the present whilst childhood memories of her father's leather jacket filled her mind. He had loved her back then and she in turn had loved him. Then because of her stubbornness and his intransigence, they had not spoken in the twelve months leading up to his death. She sighed at the memory but immediately concentrated on the question that she had been asked.

'Believe it or not I was intrigued by the work that you were doing and in particular the descriptions that you gave of Monsieur Breslin's investigations into the past. That is the sort of detective work that I would love to do. Research by computer - uncover the truth about a missing artefact and hopefully bring it to light from its hiding place. Naturally I talked about it but it wasn't until they started asking questions about his latest interest - in your emails I think that you referred to it as the 'Affair of the Diamond Necklace', that I started to be concerned. They wanted details about your work for him, where you lived and so on. That's when I decided that it was time to get out and sent you the email.'

'Hmm. The diamond necklace eh? I told Paul that it was just a story, a myth no more, but when I mentioned the tales that I had been told about our great great great grandfather, for some reason it only increased his interest. You were never interested in the family history but there are some dark secrets buried in there.'

Lillian's reply surprised him.

* * *

'I have regretted that I showed so little respect for the family. Getting caught up in this mess has made me think hard about myself. I suppose I deserve all that I got but I hate the fact that I had to involve you. You are probably a few 'greats' out but what had our ancestor got to do with the missing necklace?'

'We have very few facts. It is known that he was a lawyer around the time of the Revolution and at one time was a friend of Robespierre. The story that I was told was that he fled France but little beyond that is known for sure. He probably bought the Versailles house originally but the most intriguing thing is that in a letter that has been passed down, one that he received from a friend of his, a brief reference is made to the necklace and the inference was that he was familiar with the scandal. This is what intrigued Paul and what started him on his latest investigation. This is what he does. He has little interest in the finances and businesses that were passed on to him by the late Earl but give him a historical mystery to solve, particularly if there is a profit to be made, then he is in his element.'

Gaston paused while he concentrated on the traffic around him. By now they were on the A10 and the gap that he liked to leave before the vehicle in front of him was constantly being eaten by drivers cutting him up. He had to think when after a few minutes of silence Lillian asked, 'So what will happen to me now?'

It was another surprise as his upfront, self confident sister asked a question that just one day earlier would have been impossible for her. She was really shaken up.

'I promised that I would look after you and so I will. You

will get a second chance that you possibly don't deserve. I have plenty of money and some influential friends. One way or another we'll get this sorted. Now let me concentrate.'

Five minutes later he heard a semi snore and one glance told him that she was fast asleep.

The drive south was uneventful aside from the occasional driver that wished to get into the rear seat with them. *Why do the French have to drive so close behind* he wondered for the third time in the last hour.

At last he took the exit from the autoroute and made his way towards the village. He was fairly certain that they hadn't been followed but then there was no need for them to do so. Thanks to Lillian's loose tongue they knew where he lived and so could arrive at their leisure. Mind you the last time that they had uninvited guests it had ended badly for the visitors largely due to his two colleagues Guilbert and Patrice. Those two were the most friendly, amiable pair that you could imagine - that is until they were called into action. He could imagine that their life must seem very staid now after their time working for the French Secret Service. They both professed that it was what they wanted, to return to their home village and work quietly - one as a gardener the other as a cook to the late Earl of Strathearn. He also had seen first hand how quickly they had reverted to type last year when the home of the the Earl had been attacked. Rather than going straight back Gaston decided to stop in the village to see if he could find one or both of them. The chances would be that they would be close to the bar and the hog roast and as far away from the dancing as possible. He slowly drove into the car park on the edge of the village square and parked the car. Lillian was just waking up and she looked around with a bemused look on her face. She had lived her life in Versailles and Paris and the rural scene that she now saw was as alien to her as any foreign country.

11

Lillian stretched and opened the door of the car. She carefully got out and was surprised when she noticed the solid noise that was made when she pushed the door closed behind her. It was completely different to the tinny sound that she was used to from the friend's cars that she occasionally used. She was also conscious from the stares of the people around her that her dress was a little unusual for this part of the country. In the past she would have been disparaging about the people that looked then glanced away but she was starting to realise that perhaps it was she herself that was a little unusual. The thought crossed her mind that maybe she had known this for some time but had not been prepared to recognise the fact. Dressing and behaving as she did had been her way of shocking those around her and it was just possible that maybe she was the one that was out of kilter with the rest of the world.

* * *

Gaston was striding in the direction of the square and she had to hurry to catch up. A traditional tune that she remembered from her childhood came from the band on the makeshift stage but Gaston had changed direction and was walking towards a group of men that were stood talking, each with a plastic tumbler in their hand. A number of them shouted a greeting and he acknowledged them with a smile. He had lived and worked here for a number of years and despite his idiosyncrasies he was recognised and welcomed as one of their own. Towards the back of the crowd he could see a stocky, middle aged man whose receding hairline allowed a deep tan to add a look of outdoor solidity to his demeanour. Gaston changed direction once again and this time Patrice looked up from his conversation. Seeing Gaston hurrying towards him he made his apologies and stepped out to meet him. They were old colleagues and friends despite their contrasting backgrounds and outlook on life. Patrice was a solid, down to earth individual whereas Gaston was completely the opposite with his English affectations and slightly effeminate voice, but despite this the two had a lot of respect for each other. For a few minutes Patrice listened without interrupting whilst Gaston explained the situation to him. When Gaston had finished, Patrice then turned to Lillian and started to question her closely about the people from whom they had escaped. He grimaced slightly when she added the fact that she had told them the name of the village where her brother was living then paused for a moment to digest the information. They waited patiently until finally Patrice spoke.

'We need to contact Paul in Brittany. If he is agreeable you need to go and stay there. This mob won't know about its existence and you should be safe. I'll get hold of Guilbert and we'll sort things out here.'

* * *

Gaston had seen the outcome at first hand when once before the two men had 'sorted things out'. It had been a swift and effective defence of the chateau here in the village where they worked when it had been attacked last year. He had not asked about the disposal of the bodies that had resulted but imagined that they were experienced at cleaning up such a mess and it was certain that the deceased attackers would not have been reported as missing.

He pulled out his mobile phone and dialled Paul's number. It was answered after the first ring but he had to spend the first few minutes reassuring his employer that he was well and that there was a valid reason that he had been ignoring all of his communications. A brief conversation followed, after which he turned to Lillian and directed her back to the car. After a few more words with Patrice he turned and followed. By now he was feeling decidedly tired and tetchy. His day so far had consisted of evading criminals, driving for several hours from Versailles to the Loire region and now, he was faced with another five hours or so on the road with his sister in the passenger seat. His sister, he fumed to himself, that he had rarely heard from in over two years. He felt grimy and tired but there was no opportunity to rest or even to freshen up. They had to leave immediately in order to guarantee that they would not be seen by anyone that might have followed. It was no surprise that having caught up with Lillian he growled at her.

'If you think that you look odd here just wait until we arrive in Brittany. They will think that you have escaped from a freak show.'

Equally, it should have been no surprise when Lillian burst

into floods of tears. Except that it startled both of them. She had adopted the snide, tough facade for so long, it shocked them both when her defences finally crumbled. It didn't help that the heavy black mascara that she used washed down her face marking it with dark streaks. Despite this, Gaston was still insistent that they get moving.

'We'll stop at a service station on the way and you can sort yourself out.'

The next few hours were uneventful and somewhere near to Rennes Gaston pulled off the road. While he fuelled the car Lillian went to find a washroom. Having paid for the petrol, he moved the car into a parking bay and went into the café ordering tea for himself and a coffee for his sister. It was another fifteen minutes before she emerged and he was just starting to become concerned at her prolonged absence. He had to disguise his surprise as she slid into the seat opposite him. Not only had she washed away the dense makeup that she wore, but most of the facial piercings had gone and she had obviously managed to find a shop where she had purchased a clean white T-shirt. It was an extreme contrast to its predecessor, a ripped, black platform for the message in English 'Fuck the World - I want to get off.'

He resisted commenting, deciding instead on a less provocative description of their destination.

'You probably haven't heard of Locquirec but it's a beautiful little port on the north Breton coast. Paul was attending the funeral of his grandmother and he may have decided to stay there in order to sort out her affairs. I understand that he was her last remaining relative so there was probably a lot to do. I have been ignoring his texts, emails and calls for the last few days as you requested, but to be honest I have felt quite guilty in doing so. I loved working for the old Earl but after his death, Paul took over the businesses and asked me to step up to become in effect, his business manager. It was brave of him to do so and he would have been quite entitled to have brought in a better qualified outsider to do the job.'

'I don't understand. He inherited a multi-million euro business portfolio but asked you to manage them on his behalf. Why did he not take them on himself?'

'Paul is a historian. His passion lies in lecturing, writing and hunting down old artefacts. Last year, before the death of the Earl, the two of them traced the lineage of a pastel by Leonardo the painter from its creation right through the present day. They uncovered a host of fascinating and potentially explosive stories as a result. This is what he excels in. I was familiar with the business portfolio as the Earl would frequently talk to me about the investments that he made. So far it's working quite well and it has freed Paul to make some serious money uncovering and validating two old paintings in the last six months alone. Whilst researching this necklace business, he uncovered a link between an ancestor of ours and Marie Antoinette the wife of Louis XVI. I say a link but it is extremely tenuous. They were both in Versailles at the same time and for some reason, Antoine who would have been perhaps our great grandfather four or five times over, was forced to flee. I showed Paul a letter which has been passed down through our family which Antoine originally received from a friend in Bordeaux.'

Lillian had been listening carefully but could not resist a slight interruption by waiting for a pause then commenting, 'You weren't listening. Not four or five times removed -

more like ten or eleven.'

Gaston smiled replying, 'You were always the mathematician. I'm having to learn it as I go. Anyway, Paul got quite excited when he learned that Antoine's flight also coincided with the date of the execution of Robespierre.'

The two continued to talk surprising each other at how naturally they were able to revert back to the brother sister relationship that they had enjoyed many years ago. When eventually Gaston indicated that it was time to move, Lillian decided to head to the restroom again and Gaston stood up and walked across to the car which he had parked just outside. As he sat waiting he pondered over the events that had led to this strange and dangerous life that Lillian had been leading. Their home life had been stable and indeed, in some ways, it could have been considered privileged. Until she had reached the age of sixteen or so she had been an outgoing, vivacious teenager who was performing well at school and had a full and active social life. He himself had long ago left Versailles, initially to go to University and then to work in Paris and eventually working for William Scott, but he was in constant contact with his family and the change in Lillian's outlook and attitude had perhaps crept up without him really noticing. Then came the expulsion from school and her own exodus to the capital. By this time he was working for William Scott down in the Blois district of the Loire and with all of the events of the last two years had become somewhat wrapped up in his own world. The death of his parents in a car crash had been a shock but he had been most upset that his sister had not been bothered to attend the funeral, instead simply sending a curt message to the effect that she couldn't get away from work. Communication between the two had been sporadic at best, but for some time after the funeral Gaston had tried to keep in touch with her, sending long emails telling her about his life and work. In return he had received brief, superficial replies and eventually his efforts had petered out as he became increasingly exasperated with her. He glanced at his watch and was surprised when he noted that he had been sat in the car for more than twenty minutes. *Where has she got to?* he wondered. *Surely not buying more clothes.*

Another ten minutes passed and now Gaston was starting to worry. Surely they couldn't have been followed here. He got out of the car and started with the shop. Nothing. Café next. The same. Finally he asked an attendant to check the toilets in case she had been taken ill but again, nothing. He had just started to walk towards the petrol pumps when a vibration on his phone indicated a message coming in. It simply stated, *'No police - we'll be in contact.'* They were using Lillian's mobile.

There was no point in trying to follow them. There were a number of routes that they could take back to Paris from here, even if they didn't go across country.

What is it, he thought, *that they want from her, that made abduction an acceptable option.*

Ten minutes later and both Patrice and Paul had been alerted to the situation. Both had given their reassurances and both had suggested that his best option was to carry on to Locquirec and to wait there for further contact from them. It was a long worrying journey along the N12 and then down the back roads that led to the coast. Eventually, he turned right at the roundabout on the edge of the town and down into the old port itself. There were plenty of parking spaces and he pulled into one of them and turned off the engine. On a different day and under different circumstances, he acknowledged to himself, this would have been a beautiful setting. The tide was out but a small empty beach stretched out in front of him. To his left was a harbour wall and small fishing boats were anchored out near the entrance. Across the bay he could see more beaches that were backed by green countryside. The view probably hadn't changed in the last fifty years. He turned around and could see a crêperie and café which were wedged in by several colourful old cottages - obviously modernised and in use as holiday homes.

It was from the café that Paul stood up and walked over to greet him. It was only a year ago that the two had first met, but in that time their relative circumstances had changed and because of his inheritance Paul was now his employer, albeit a very generous and trusting one. In spite of this relationship, the two had become very good friends although a very British shake of the hand was all that passed between them. Gaston had never been fond of the French 'bise' - the air kiss and preferred to use the Anglo Saxon greeting whenever possible.

I had been waiting for Gaston to arrive wondering what all of this was about. He looked shaken by the events of the day and after he shook my hand I asked,

'Do you want a coffee or would you prefer to walk?'

After he had spent so many hours in the car the answer was obvious so I directed him towards a path that led away to the right of the harbour. As we walked, Gaston gave me more details about the events that had occurred during the course of what was turning out to be a very long day.

* * *

'I can't understand how they found us at that service station unless they had followed us. And for how long? From Blois? From Paris?   And I just don't understand what they want with Lillian. They had scared her enough that there was no chance that she was going to the police if they left her alone. I'm worried that they think there is only one way of ensuring her silence.'

I had been thinking the same thing but tried to reassure Gaston as best I could.

'The text that they sent after they took her suggests otherwise. I'm afraid that there are only two things that we can do. Firstly I'll ask Patrice and Guilbert to use their contacts to try to find them and then we just wait to see what it is they want.'

The footpath soon ran down to a shingle beach but just before it did so there was a bench which overlooked the bay. It was another sunny evening and we sat for a few minutes watching the small boats dancing on the water.

'So what has been happening here? I have been so wrapped up in my own problems I forgot to ask.   Unforgivable.' Gaston shook his head slowly.

'It's OK - you're forgiven' I joked. 'The simple answer is quite a lot. The funeral was quite emotional as you would expect. Alicia came down from Paris but had to return the next day. Oh - and I suspect that I have been left the house in grandmother's will.'

'So what will you do? Sell it or rent it out?'

* * *

'Ah - here's the thing. I'm seriously thinking about moving in. William's place has never really felt like home and I much prefer the area here to the Loire valley. Depending on what you, Patrice and Guilbert decide, I would like to keep the place back there as a sort of business headquarters but carry out my own work from this house in Locquirec. Even out on the headland where it's located I can get a good mobile signal and I will have satellite internet installed. Basically I would like you three to continue as you were but I would simply relocate to Brittany. Obviously you will want to talk it through with them and I will wait anyway until we have sorted out this awful business. OK - enough shocks and surprises for one day. Let's go back to the car and drive round to the house. I'll set up one of the guest rooms for you. I have advertised for someone to come in once a week to do a bit of cleaning but until I have got that sorted out we are on our own.'

'But what about Lillian? Maybe it's time to go to the police.'

'From what you described I would hold fire a little to see what they want. It may be that we can get her back without risking her future.'

'I agree but the first indication that things are going badly and we get some extra help. Anyway, I have to say that I have far more faith in Patrice and Guilbert and their contacts than I have in the gendarmerie.'

With that agreement we strode back to my car and within ten minutes were negotiating the track that led to what I hoped would be my new domain. Despite his grim demeanour Gaston admired the way that the house dominated the headland and the arresting view that it commanded.

'So, Alicia stayed overnight did she? Such a nice girl. It's a pity you don't see more of her.'

My reply was simple and to the point. 'Mind your own bloody business.'

It had been an exhausting day for Gaston so he retired early. I went up to the top room and tried the window. The hinges were corroded after many years of exposure to the salt that was carried in the blown sea spray but eventually it creaked open. Outside, peeling wooden shutters were fastened back against the wall. Goodness knows how they were accessed at this height. The floor to ceiling calico curtains wafted in the late evening breeze filtering the light from the setting sun. In stark contrast to the reality of the situation, it made for a calm and pleasant atmosphere. Despite my love of modern technology I liked to go old school whilst sketching out ideas and my habit was to pull out one of the many notebooks that I used. I started to draw a timeline of the events that Gaston had described, but when I had finished I still had no inkling of the reason for this kidnap. I was still pretty sure that there would be contact from them but if nothing had arrived by tomorrow then it would definitely be passed on to the police.

The next morning I was up bright and early and walked into the village to buy some croissants for breakfast. After we had eaten I left Gaston to explore and I went back up to what I was starting to call my study. I really would be disappointed if this house didn't become mine. I flipped open the MacBook lid and scanned my emails again. It must have been the fifth time that morning but this time success. I read through the email quickly the first time then more carefully the second. It had been sent from an anonymous gmail account but I guessed that anyone who knew about these things would be able to trace its origin. And I knew such a person. That however, was for later. I needed to locate Gaston as it seemed that his help would be needed immediately.

The problem with living in a big house is that it's big and trying to find somebody can turn into a bit of an expedition. I considered the problem for a moment then thought, 'What the hell' and hollered at the top of my voice. I heard a reply in the distance. OK - narrowed it down. It sounded as though his voice had carried in through the window. Outside then. Two minutes later I met him at the front door and suggested that we go back outside. Gaston did well in trying to hide his anxiety but his relief when I told him that I had received an email and that Lillian was alive and well was palpable. It was then that he started to receive a sequence of texts that he grimly read out as they arrived.

12

David Motte had lived all of his life in Paris to the extent that the rest of the world held little interest for him. A middle aged man with an instantly forgettable face, that is apart from the small veins that could be seen around his nose, the result of an indulgence for rather expensive oak aged Burgundy wine. Brought up in a relatively poor family, with pretensions way beyond their income, he had finally broken free by buying and selling art works to wealthy Parisian clients who had much more money than good sense. He was a mild man who, unless severely provoked, was incapable of carrying out any act of aggression. Of course there was no need to do so when he could simply pay others to do it for him. Lucrative as the art market was, he actually made the majority of his income by paying naive teenagers to write malware that once installed onto a person's computer or mobile phone, waited until that person opened an online banking program and then transmitted the login data to his own system. Thus, thousands of private bank accounts had been emptied and the contents electronically transferred via a random series of intermediary accounts to their final resting place. The transactions were untraceable and David Motte was steadily accumulating a small fortune.

His was a strange background in that his parents had lived on an income that allowed them to survive in the family home in the suburbs of Paris but were unable to replace anything that became shabby or worn out. The story that they told was that the Motte family line was descended from the 'De La Mottes' who could be traced back to the 18th Century before the Revolution had taken place. It was believed that the downward spiral from riches and wealth into the current relative poverty had started with the disappearance of Nicholas De La Motte who had been searching for a diamond necklace that family history related was rightfully theirs. The fact that the 'Affair of the Queen's Necklace' was well documented and that in fact the part played by Nicholas had been less than honest seemed to have been missed by the current family members. Even so it had been ingrained into him since early childhood that the necklace had been wrongly taken away from them.

Whilst at university at the Sorbonne, he had crossed paths with a flamboyant character who went by the name of Gaston Lestrade. His interest had been kindled when he realised that this man was possibly the descendant of one of the characters that had entered his own family history. Blurred by the centuries and multiple retellings, a Lestrade with the first name of Antoine, it was believed, had somehow been involved in the death of Nicholas De La Motte although the exact details were never made clear. By extension they also believed that the Lestrade family were partly to blame for the decline of the Motte dynasty. Of course if Gaston had even been aware of the existence of David Motte and had heard this story for himself, he would have laughed and ridiculed the tale. As it was, Gaston's circle of friends was of a totally different ilk to that of David Motte's and consequently the two had never met.

Sadly, David Motte believed this version of his family history to be true and had followed Gaston's progress obsessively. In an attempt to break away from the families spiral of decline he had been determined to become rich by whatever means possible and when he was able to sell a third rate daub that he had acquired in a flea market at a vastly inflated price to a gullible acquaintance, his path was set. It was no coincidence that when Lillian had left home under something of a cloud it was David Motte that had offered her work and ensured that her illegal hacking on his behalf had been well documented. At that point, he wasn't sure how he could use this fortunate occurrence but he would be ready when the time came.

Now, once again, Lillian was sat opposite him although this time there were some differences in her appearance. The outlandish makeup that she habitually wore had gone and the T-shirt was plain white and no longer bearing an offensive message. However, his plan was now back on track.

His voice was soft when he spoke. ' Before you start on one of your tirades my dear, let me remind you that you are here of your own volition and that you are free to walk out at any time. The result of such an action before I am ready however, would be unfortunate. The dossier that I would be forced to release to the police is extensive and contains details not only of your actual work but additional hacks that I have attributed to you. I would guess that the result would be a long, long period of incarceration. '

Sensibly, Lillian held back for a moment before simply replying. ' So what is it that you want? What do I have to do to get my freedom back.'

' What I want is simply an exchange. You mentioned that your brother's employer was looking into your family history and in particular to a connection with the missing diamond necklace that belonged to Marie Antoinette. That necklace in fact belongs to my family. I want it back.'

The expression of incredulity that passed across Lillian's face stopped him for a moment but then he continued.

'You need to persuade this Paul Breslin that your welfare is closely linked to his research into the matter. I am certain that the necklace has been hidden somewhere as there has been no mention of it throughout history since it disappeared from the Queen's summer palace just after her execution. When he finds it and hands it to me, I will have no more need of your file and it will be destroyed.'

Lillian wasn't sufficiently naive to believe that he would destroy the only copy but as she listened to him, she realised that there was no point in bringing it up at the moment. That would be a conversation for another day. However, there was one problem. This man believed in the existence of an artefact that had disappeared over two hundred years ago and her best chance of freedom relied on it being found. She had little choice but to go along with him for the time being.

* * *

'All right, what do you want me to do first? Presumably you are going to contact Gaston again and explain to him what you have just told me.'

'I will explain the situation and then you are going to speak to him later. It really is in your very best interest to persuade him that I am serious.'

'And what if it doesn't exist or can't be found?'

'It does exist and you had better hope that this Paul Breslin is as good as his reputation suggests. I have arranged for a guest room to be set up for you. You are welcome to use the library and the garden. There will be no mobile or internet connection for you I'm afraid and if you step outside the grounds I will assume that it is a breach of our agreement and your file would be sent to an interested party that I know. Food will be served to you in the suite that is adjacent to the bedroom. I will send for you when I am ready.'

As soon as he had finished speaking, a tall, short haired man wearing what looked liked a very expensive suit appeared from a door to her right and indicated that she should walk in front of him.

Stepping into a long corridor she spoke over her shoulder.

'That's a good trick if you can pull it off. Unfortunately I saw the sensor that Motte activated to signal you. Simple electronics only looks impressive to the uninitiated. Do you have a name by the way? If I am to be stuck here for a while, I need to call you something.'

'Keep walking and turn left at the bottom of the corridor. I doubt that you will see me again so there is no need for names.'

Lillian shrugged her shoulders and following the directions soon found herself walking through a room that under different circumstances would have a been an extremely comfortable place to have spent a few days. There was a large picture window looking out onto a terraced garden. The room itself was mainly decorated in white and contained a large TV in one corner. A bookcase stood against one wall and a large chesterfield sofa was situated next to another. In front of the window a table and single chair were obviously set up for her to be able to dine in relative comfort. A door opposite to the one through which she had entered presumably led into the bedroom. *All in all*, she thought, *it could have been much worse.*

But a moment later reflected. *Who am I kidding? Even if this necklace exists, it could take months to locate it.*

It was not long after this that David Motte was using her mobile phone to send a detailed set of demands to Gaston. Like most people, Lillian was not a brave person and when they had demanded that she switch off the fingerprint sensor and give up the 4 digit pass code she had quickly obliged. He was uncertain as to Gaston's location at this point but it made little difference to his plans. He already had people located close to Montignac and when Gaston and Lillian had driven south from Paris, it was a simple matter for them to watch and then follow. Why they had then left the village and driven towards Rennes was a mystery but a simple phone call had instructed his men to follow them and to take the girl when it became possible. In any case the actual location of Gaston Lestrade was irrelevant. He needed him to persuade his employer Paul Breslin that the threats towards Lillian were serious and that their best hope lay with him locating the necklace and handing it over. It was now a matter of waiting and seeing what transpired. If the necklace genuinely couldn't be located by one of the best art and history detectives in Europe, then a worst case scenario would be to let the girl go but to keep the file on her as insurance to make sure that she kept her mouth shut. He really couldn't lose either way but there was a chance that he might gain possession of an artefact that should be worth millions.

On the other side of the luxurious townhouse Lillian was thinking. Once the shock of her abduction had died down she had sat and thought through the situation and had satisfied herself that she was in no immediate danger. If anything had been going to happen to her it would have happened by now. The story that he had told her was something of a surprise - not because of its origin in the eighteenth century but because of his ludicrous claim to the ownership of the necklace. She had never associated his name with the infamous Jeanne and Nicholas de la Motte of the story but it seemed a reasonable connection. The 'Affair of the Diamond Necklace' was well known in France and had been taught as part of the history of the Revolution back in school. It was generally considered that the two were mere confidence tricksters and had been found out but had fled leaving Marie Antoinette to shoulder the anger of the population. She wondered what sort of twisted logic though, should lead David Motte to believe that it rightfully belonged to his family. It was an even bigger step to believe that the necklace could still be found. True it had disappeared but the story was so well known that if it had subsequently reappeared on the open market it would have been well documented. So, for her, a worse case scenario was being stuck here and then being able to get on with her life. Except that possession of the file might allow him to ensure that she had to continue to work for him. If she was to get herself sorted out, all copies of the file had to be destroyed and her best chance of doing that was while she was here in the house. The problem was, she had no access to a computer of any kind. It was one to think about but in the meantime, she was bored. Gaston had once chided her with the phrase, 'only boring people get bored' but she hadn't believed it then and she didn't believe it now. She rarely watched TV and a bookcase full of books about history and antiques didn't fill her with enthusiasm.

And so it was when the door to her quarters opened and an elderly lady appeared with a food tray, she adopted her most abject and pathetic voice and asked if she would be allowed access to pens and notebooks. The woman placed the tray on her table and simply replied that she would pass the message on. She left immediately leaving Lillian to realise just how hungry she was. Taking the lid from the dish revealed a beautiful looking cassoulet which she immediately spooned out and devoured.

An hour later the old lady re-appeared to remove the tray and without speaking simply placed a black pocket sized notebook with a rollerball pen on the table in front of Lillian. While she had been considering her limited options earlier an inkling of an idea had occurred to her but it was complex and she needed help in shaping it. The pen and paper were a bit old school but under the circumstances they were the only tools to which she could get access.

It was difficult to believe that it was only this morning that she had been chased across Versailles, driven south for three hours then another two hours towards Brittany before being abducted and brought back to Paris. How boredom had ever entered her thoughts she really couldn't now envisage and with the germ of a plan in place she would be fully occupied during the coming days.

At about the same time that Lillian was eating, David Motte was sat in his extensive office mulling over the events of the day. He had contacted both Gaston Lestrade and his employer Paul Breslin and was pretty sure of their cooperation. As long as Lestrade's sister faced the prospect of a long term prison sentence, he was confident that they would do all that they could to find the necklace. He was surprised to hear that Lillian had asked for pen and paper but there was no reason that he could think of to refuse the request. In any case, he had cleverly given a notebook rather than loose sheets. That way he could easily see what she was doing with them and it would be impossible to hide anything. All in all it had been a good day. The only down side had been the two idiots that had been caught in the grounds of the Versailles Palace carrying guns. However, they had been hired through a proxy and could not be traced back to him. Yes, all in all it had been a good day.

He turned back to the computer screen and opened the file manager. Everything was arranged logically, one area set aside for his legitimate work, buying and selling works of art and another for the shadier side of his life. Keeping track of all of the malware applications that he had instigated and the consequent income stream that they generated required organisation but this was something on which he prided himself. He also made sure that everything was backed up in cloud storage just in case of any problems occurring with the hardware in front of him. Putting thoughts of Lillian and the necklace to one side, he concentrated on his legitimate income generation from the previous trimester. Even this area of his life wasn't entrusted to an accountant but it did mean that the periodic tax forms that arrived had to be dealt with by himself. He was aware of the number of criminals that had been caught by filing incorrect tax information so even though it was an irritation he made sure that his records were meticulous. The darker side of things though, of course, were carefully hidden. Compartmentalising his life was a skill that he had developed over the years and for the next two hours he became, in his own mind, a legitimate art dealer complying with the laws of the land.

He was more than surprised when the phone that he had taken from Lillian came to life. He was even more surprised at the demands made by the caller. After the conversation finished and he put the mobile phone down on the desk he sat back and started to think. Despite his annoyance at the tone that had been taken he could see that the caller had made a valid point. However, it was a problem for tomorrow. The immediate concerns were these confounded tax forms. Compartmentalisation - to divide into compartments - and this compartment had to be closed before the next one engaged his attention.

13

Shortly after I told Gaston about the email that I had received things started to get busy. First of all a series of text messages arrived and then Gaston's phone rang and he had a brief conversation with Lillian herself.

'He really has us over a barrel. If we move against him my sister will be locked away for years. Do you think that you can find this mysterious object that he was talking about?'

I thought carefully before answering. 'We have to try. I think that it is highly improbable that the necklace still exists. The chances are that it was broken up years ago otherwise it would have been documented somewhere but this man Motte must be aware of this. He must have a contingency plan in case we fail. I would guess his best bet would be to let Lillian go free but keep the file on her as a safeguard. However, there is little that we can do apart from try to establish a trail from its creation in 1785 and try to find out what actually did happen to it.'

'You know that it was really the scandal that this thing caused that precipitated the execution of Marie Antoinette. Everybody in France knows the story. Most believe that she was in fact the victim of a very elaborate hoax and never actually received the necklace. There are a small number of us that think that she was much cleverer than she led people to believe and that the necklace was really in her possession at the summer house in Versailles. If you uncover the full story, it might give an idea as to what eventually happened to it.'

I have to admit I was intrigued by the story anyway and Gaston's vague connection with it only piqued my interest further. Even if we weren't being pressured by this clown in Paris and needed to help Lillian I still think that it was worth a little time and effort on our part. I sensed a new book could be somewhere down the line if I could sell the idea to the publishers. However, I needed somewhere to start and the only tangible evidence that we had so far was the letter that had been passed down to Gaston. So that was my next question.

'It's with my things back at the Chateau in the Loire. I could drive there now, stay overnight, brief Patrice and Guilbert and return tomorrow. Think if there is anything that you need me to bring back for you.'

'There are a few bits that you could collect for me but tell them to use their contacts in Paris discreetly, to see if they can get any information on this character Motte. I have more faith in their secret service friends than I have in the French police. In the meantime, I need to start some research into eighteenth century Versailles.'

Gaston had only been gone for an hour when I received another email, this time with an attachment. Motte it seemed had also been scouring through his family treasures and had uncovered a letter that he had photographed and attached.

I translated it into English and changed those irritating f's to s's. The letter read as follows.

2 August 1794
  My Dearest Wife

I find myself in the strangest of circumstances here in the town of Rouen. I'm not sure what will happen during the coming days so I am taking this opportunity to bring you up to date with proceedings. As you know I have been watching Lestrade very closely. As we suspected he might, he has fled to this port with the intention of leaving for the American Colonies. I confronted him today and under duress, he admitted that the necklace was in his possession. I meet him again tonight in order to regain what should rightfully be ours. If all goes well I shall return to Paris tomorrow or the day after. However, I suspect that he may try to flee again, in which case, I will follow him to the ends of the earth if necessary. If this is the case I will write again when the opportunity arises.

Nicholas

This was exciting stuff. I needed to persuade Motte to let me see the original letter in order to verify its authenticity but assuming that this had indeed been written in 1794 it established a link between Nicholas De La Motte and Antoine Lestrade. It was amazing to think that the family had harboured this so called grudge for over two hundred years but only now had action of any kind been taken. It must have been festering within the Motte family all of this time, assuming of course that the current day Motte was indeed a descendent of the De La Motte's. At this stage, it was largely irrelevant - it was enough that Motte believed it to be true and was prepared to go to such extreme lengths to try to retrieve the necklace.

There was one problem however. When Gaston had shown me his letter a few weeks before, there was a fleeting reference to Porto in Portugal and no mention of the American Colonies. This was a discrepancy that needed to be sorted out immediately. One of the documents must be wrong and I thought I knew which one it was. In Gaston's version, the author had been surprised by Antoine's location suggesting that he had landed in a place other than that intended. If true, this gave us an edge on Motte as he had obviously been looking in the wrong country. No surprise then that he had been unsuccessful. I needed to look at the letter again but at least it seemed to be a starting point. I hadn't said anything to Gaston but at the back of my mind I was wondering if I could stay ahead of Motte but still keep feeding him out of date information. In the meantime my hopes rested with Guilbert and Patrice. I was more than happy to retain them at the Chateau for their contacts as much as anything else.

The rest of the day passed without incident. Me in the study upstairs (or at least hopefully soon to be my study), window wide open whilst being distracted by the sound of the waves on the rocks below. I was reasonably familiar with the period of time in question, but there were some details that were a little hazy with which I needed to reacquaint myself. Not surprisingly there was a lot of hearsay surrounding many of the events at the time and I needed to track down primary source evidence in order to establish a timeline into which I could fit Antoine Lestrade and Nicholas De La Motte. I really needed to get my stuff in here but first I had to establish that I in fact owned the house. The will was due to be declared the following week but I couldn't wait that long. It was being held by the local notaire who I had met briefly at the funeral. He was a long time friend of my grandmother so I suspected that a visit that afternoon might at least put my mind at rest. I wasn't really concentrating on the task that I had set myself so I closed the window, set off down the stairs and locked the front door. It was much greyer and cooler today so I had pulled on a cord jacket that I liked and wrapped a scarf around my neck before striding out along the smugglers path that ran alongside the house and back towards the town. It was still lunchtime so there was no chance of finding the man in his office just yet. People think that two hour lunch breaks make the French a lazy nation but they don't realise that it is not uncommon for them to work into the evening. Anyway, it gave me an excuse to stop at the bar in the port and order a café noisette. Basically an espresso with just a hint of milk, it got its name from its nutty colour and had long ago become my coffee of choice. Not that there was a lot of choice in France - for a food loving nation they were still a long way behind Italy in the range of coffees. It was tourist season but I was still able to find a table on the veranda overlooking the bay. I habitually carried a pocket notebook with me and whilst I waited for the waitress I started to jot down what I actually knew about the events of August 1794.

1. *Middle of French Revolution*

2. *Five years after storming of Bastille*

3. *28th July Robespierre executed*

4. *2nd August Letter from Nicholas De La Motte to his wife - hastily written from Rouen.*

5. *2nd August Antoine Lestrade in Rouen if letter to be believed. Planning to escape to the American Colonies.*

It occurred to me that it would have taken them several days to get from Versailles to Rouen. Was it possible that the journey was instigated by Robespierre's bloody end. It seemed an unlikely coincidence but the dates were very significant. It was all very tenuous but it was a start. If Motte was to be believed it would seem that Antoine had the necklace in his possession at this point - but where had he got it from? The Queen was locked away in Paris and it hadn't even been established that she had the necklace herself. Perhaps Antoine had stolen it from Motte. Thinking it through this seemed the most likely conclusion and made more sense of the letter. I needed to see Gaston's letter in order to corroborate some of these details but I was pretty sure that it had references to Portugal rather than the Colonies. I was starting to put together a plan that might take us forward but I would have to wait for the return of Gaston the next day before I could start. Meanwhile, it was time to go to see the Notaire. Just an hour later I was back home having had unofficial confirmation that I was indeed the new owner of this massive old building. Just over a year ago, I was a fairly successful historian with a reasonable but not excessive income. On the rare occasions when I moved house I did most of the work that was involved by myself. OK - I would bring in a decorator to paint the walls and so on but the rest of the stuff was down to me. Now, because of a sequence of events that had been nothing to do with me I was wealthy enough to be able pay someone to set this place up in just the way that I would want it. That was for the future, however, in the short term I could live with my grandmother's tastes - except for the study. I wanted my antique desk in front of the window, my old malacca silver tipped cane which was a legacy of a motorcycle accident, hung on the wall and a satellite dish feeding a reasonable if somewhat laggy broadband. My library of books, chesterfield chair and my streaming sound system would complete the study. The rest of the house could wait. I had a feeling that I would be fully occupied during the coming few weeks, largely I told myself, trying to help Gaston and his sister, but secretly trying to solve this mystery to my own satisfaction. After all a local artist Paul Cezanne famously came to the conclusion that it's not really possible to help others. They need to do it for themselves. I didn't necessarily agree but I had to admit to myself that the extra motivation of solving another historical mystery was an added incentive for me. Did that make me a bad person?

The rest of the day disappeared quickly. I had a flurry of emails to answer and I spent a long period of time on my iPhone persuading a local firm that I really needed that satellite dish urgently and couldn't wait for the two weeks that they were suggesting. They were obviously on some kind of sales bonus so when I indicated that I was signing up for the top of the range data package they suddenly became much more accommodating. Yes tomorrow was no problem at all, they could call in at the end of the day on the way back from another job. Eventually, I decided that enough was enough and a walk was in order. Locking up I turned left out of the gate and walked along the headland to the bay, then turned left again into town and soon found myself back in the port. I use the term port loosely as most of the vessels were either leisure craft or small fishing boats. It really was a lovely place and I was becoming quite excited at the thought of it becoming my new home. I suddenly realised that I hadn't eaten all day so once again I sat down at the café/bar and ordered a bowl of mussels and a carafe of sauvignon blanc. Later, as I retraced my steps home, I was able to watch the lights across the bay reflecting on the water. What a set of mixed emotions - happiness at my location, sadness about my grandmother and concern for Gaston and his sister. Time to check on progress I supposed and reaching my study I opened the window wide and dialled the number of Lillian's phone that I had recorded after the text messages had arrived earlier. It was getting late and judging by the surprised response I guessed that Motte was shocked that I had the temerity to contact him. He had laid out his terms earlier in the day so now it was my turn.

'Good evening Mr Motte. Please don't bother trying to bluster - you have threatened my business manager and his sister so I have a few things to say to you. First of all, if she is mistreated in any way the police will be the least of your worries. If you have done your homework correctly, you will be aware of my connections with the French anti-terrorist squad. Trust me when I say that they are people that you do not want to get involved with. I am prepared to carry out this farcical search of yours for a necklace that almost certainly no longer exists but be aware that I am also doing it for my own interest. Whether I find it or not, and I am fairly positive that I won't, I expect that the file on Lillian will be handed over. Of course you will keep copies but if they are ever used there will be a cost to you.'

At this point I realised that the half litre of wine was possibly contributing to some of the empty threats that I was making but, as they say, 'God loves a trier.'

* * *

I decided that I might as well push my luck a little further.

'As you have this so called file as leverage there seems to be no point in keeping her captive. Before I lift a finger I insist that she is allowed to leave Paris. At the very least her computer skills might be useful in tracking down any documents that I need.'

I thought I heard a snort on the other end of the line as I waited for a reply.

'Mr. Breslin, that necklace belongs to my family by right and I will use all of my considerable wealth to get it back by any means available to me. I will consider your request for the return of the girl but do remember the file. If I release it there will be a lengthy prison sentence for her. As for the rest of your threats, I suspect that they lie on fallow ground. I will be in contact tomorrow. Good night'.

Enough for tonight I decided. I really must get my music server and system set up here as soon as possible. A touch of Eric Satie wouldn't go amiss at the moment. Mind you, some clean clothes would be more practical. I had been here longer than I planned already and to be honest I couldn't see myself leaving in the immediate future. Oh well, Gaston would be back tomorrow. If I get Lillian back here I would guess that he might want to stay for the duration so his organisational skills can get this place set up for me. There are certainly more than enough guest rooms. It was fairly obvious that this room had been little used for some time - probably too many flights of stairs as she became older and more frail. I sat down on the only seat left up here listening to the waves below then cursed as my iPhone rang again. Glancing at the caller id, I was surprised to see it was Patrice. He rarely used his mobile phone so I was a little concerned and answered immediately. His opening of 'Evening boss,' relaxed me though and I listened carefully to what he had to say. The gist of it was that after Gaston's arrival, he had immediately spoken to his friends in Paris and they had quickly come up with a background check on Motte.

'Let Guilbert and I pay him a visit and I guarantee that he will soon let the girl go.'

I explained that I hoped she would be released anyway and that at the moment, force would be counterproductive. This bloody file was always going to be the problem. It was a moments work to make multiple copies of electronic data so there was never going to be a guarantee that we had all of them.

'For the time being, we wait. If she is released tomorrow I carry on with the search which will gain us some time and perhaps enable us to come up with an alternative plan.'

I think that Patrice was joking when he suggested that a nudge in the back as the metro train approached might solve the problem. I wasn't risking it so a firm no from me evoked a chortle before he wished me good night.

14

I woke the next morning to dark clouds and squalls of rain that were sweeping in from the North. It had become my habit to leave the curtains and shutters open so that as soon as I opened my eyes I could decide what to put on for that day - except for the fact that my choice was limited to what I had brought in my suitcase for a few days stay. I sighed and after emerging from the shower sniffed at my shirt trying to ignore the slightly acrid aroma that it gave off. Fortunately, the Levi's that I had travelled in were still serviceable and as yet I had not spilled anything on the sweater that had been in use for almost a week. The kitchen was on the ground floor so that was my first stop for coffee. I had bought a serviceable filter machine two days ago and although it wasn't capable of pressurising the powder to make an espresso, the coffee that it produced was surprisingly good. I opened the door that led into the garden and watched the clouds exchanging position with patches of blue sky that occasionally but temporarily appeared. Even if Gaston had set off as soon as it was light he wouldn't be here for several hours so I grabbed my jacket and set off to make inroads into my 10000 steps for the day. It was a number that had been recommended by some research in the US, somewhat at random I suspected as I seldom seemed to reach it but at least it was a target and gave me an excuse, as if I needed one, to explore this beautiful coastline. Today I turned right and followed the path around the headland and into the port, this time continuing my walk through the boat launching area, past a number of houses that looked over the bay to a bench that was positioned next to a pebble beach. It was damp but as the rain had temporarily stopped I sat down and pulled out my notebook. Yesterday I had started listing what I knew about the events of 1794 and it only took me a few seconds to look over them. After a little bit of research last night I was able to add the following.

- *The French Republic abolished slavery.*

- *The scientist Lavoisier was guillotined sometime in May.*

- *France seemed to be at war with the rest of Europe. (At this time, Napoleon was just a seemingly successful officer in the French army. It would be a few years before he came to power).*

What an incongruous selection of events was my first thought. Abolishing slavery and yet murder and war. It was a period of history that had largely passed me by but there was obviously much more going on than I had first thought. Much for me to learn and probably then much more to be researched. I was a great believer that art was often a window into a time period and as an art historian, I was starting to think that this might be one of several starting points. I had been often told that an unfortunate habit of mine was that of being single track minded. Whilst I focused on one thing the rest of the world might as well not exist. I say frequently noted but in fact it was a character trait that had been mainly picked up by past girlfriends. My defence had always been that they had not complained whilst they were the focus of my attention - just when they were not. As I looked around I realised that today was probably the crunch time for Lillian. If Motte had seriously taken note of my tirade yesterday it made no sense to hang on to her for any longer. I hoped that he saw the sense of what I had said and that we wouldn't have to worry about her wellbeing after today. Even if she was released it wouldn't make a jot of difference to the fact that her real problem lay with her past and with this file that Motte professed to have put together. In his position I would have done the same so the sensible thing would be to carry on with the investigation and see what transpired in the meantime. Of course, as I have said before, I was now sufficiently intrigued to pursue this necklace whether or not there was that added leverage. I stood up, grimacing at the damp patch on my trousers from the wet bench and turned back towards town.

Back in the house in the suburbs of Paris it was after nine and Lillian had breakfasted well. The juice was fresh and the coffee was strong. This was good, but of much more importance to her she had a plan. Admittedly, it was only the grain of an idea but she hated the feeling of helplessness that came with her situation. The last few days had really shaken her and it was obvious to her that her rebellious days were over. Well at least mostly over. As soon as this was concluded she needed to realign her life. The croissant on her plate was almost finished when the door opened again and this time it was Motte that appeared and spoke.

'Get your things. You're moving. We leave in half an hour.'

Not waiting to hear a reply, he closed the door and left.

She had started to use the notebook that she had been given but to the uninitiated it would appear to contain just a random collection of words and symbols. It had been examined on several occasions but simply given back to her with a shrug. She slipped it into her pocket and stood up.

Where now, she thought. *Wherever it is, it won't be as comfortable or convenient as this place. Oh well, hope for the best but prepare for the worst. The trouble is - there's nothing I can do to prepare for anything.*

Exactly thirty minutes after the visit from Motte, the same man that had escorted her the previous day appeared and gestured for her to follow him. He was as taciturn as the first time and simply ignored all of her questions about where they were going. A large black Peugeot was parked outside the front door with another one of Motte's employees ready to get into the driver's seat. Her escort indicated that she was to sit in the back and then sat down next to her. Lillian was now starting to feel concerned. Logically, she reasoned, there was no reason that she should come to any harm but this was starting to feel increasingly sinister.

Before long, they were entering the Périphérique, the notorious ring road around Paris and as usual the traffic was almost at a standstill. After thirty minutes during which they only managed a few kilometres they turned off and Lillian was slightly startled to see the signpost for Versailles. Soon afterwards they drove along the familiar Boulevard and into the underground car park that she had left in such a hurry. When the car pulled into a parking bay she was ordered to remain where she was while the driver left the car and walked towards the lift. Two hours then passed while the man next to her sat staring at the screen of his mobile phone.

Two hours can drag when you are unoccupied but eventually she saw the driver walking back towards them. He opened the door and simply shook his head at her escort.

'I didn't expect anything else. OK - you - out.'

The door was locked from the inside so she had to wait for the driver to walk back and open her door. As she stepped out she was astonished to see the driver get back into the car, start the engine and start to pull away. The window wound down and the man in the back seat looked directly at her saying, 'The boss told me to remind you that although we don't want you anymore it is in your best interests to get Breslin moving more quickly.'

With that, the car left her standing in astonishment.

What the hell am I supposed to do now? Lillian wondered. *No phone, no keys, no money. I can't use the side entrance without my keys and I'm not even sure that the concierge will recognise me. However, the only option that I have is to try to persuade him to at least ring Gaston for permission to let me up to the flat.*

And so fifteen minutes later she found herself pleading her case with the doorman.

'OK - if you won't let me up, at least ring my brother who

will confirm that I am who I say I am.'

To his credit the man only took a few moments to retrieve Gaston's number and enter it into the phone. It was answered almost immediately and after listening carefully, he handed it across to Lillian. The relief in her brother's voice was palpable but his instructions were simple. Stay in the apartment until she was collected. Do not leave under any circumstances. And so, a few minutes later, the door to the top floor family home was being unlocked and as soon as the concierge had left she turned all of the locks and put up the chain. Despite the outward appearance of confidence and bravado Lillian had been very very scared. She had heard stories of what could happen to the people who crossed Nicholas Motte and although his mild manners and bland appearance gave a contrary impression she had certainly been concerned for her well being, particularly in the hours after she had been taken. She was puzzled by her release but was certainly not going to argue about it. There would be a number of hours before anyone arrived to collect her so in the meantime, she had work to do.

Gaston pressed the button to disconnect the call and turned to Paul, a relieved smile on his face. Paul had followed their side of the conversation so it was no surprise when Gaston simply said, 'You did it, she's free.'

After a brief discussion they both agreed that the next step was for Patrice and Guilbert to drive up to Versailles and bring Lillian back to Locquirec. If Motte did change his mind, which was a possibility given his unpredictable nature, then the two men were easily capable of dealing with it. Additionally, one advantage they had was that Motte was unaware of this location in Brittany. He believed that the chateau in the Loire was where they could be found so if direct contact were to be made, that would be his target. Unlike Gaston, Patrice and Guilbert had the training and skills to make sure that they would not be followed.

Gaston looked happier than I had seen him for a while. 'It looks as though we have a wait ahead of us. It will take them at least three hours to get to Lillian and then probably another five or so to get here. I don't know what you want to do but I have work ahead. If you have time to spare, I would be grateful if you could organise the relocation for me. The sooner I have everything here the sooner I will be comfortable. I want to get started on this research. If I can convince Motte that the necklace doesn't exist he may well leave us alone.'

Gaston frowned before replying. 'I somehow doubt that. As long as he has this leverage, I won't feel comfortable. While you follow up the eighteenth century I'll get started on organising your move. If you are happy I can work from down here - there are a number of calls that I need to make and you will work better without my voice in the background. Also it might be better for me to stay and if you can put up with her, I would be more comfortable if Lillian was here as well.'

'There's plenty of room. If you wouldn't mind organising that as well I'm going to get started.'

With that I set off for the top floor leaving Gaston to go to war on his mobile phone. Opening the door of the study a few minutes later I paused to catch my breath and gazed out through the large picture windows. I wanted to hear the sound of the sea on the rocks so I pulled the window ajar and settled down at the old table. I was starting with a limited amount of information but at least there was something there. I had names and dates and I surmised that the hunt would be similar to many that I had carried out before. No doubt there would be red herrings along the way but as long as documentation existed then I would find it. In my mind I had planned out a preliminary pattern of searches that I need to follow through, some of them here in France and others further afield. Just how far afield, however, depended on what I found out initially. Gaston had handed over a box of family papers when he had arrived back and my first job was to go through them looking for anything that mentioned Antoine Lestrade by name or anything that was dated before say about 1850. The letter that he had shown me previously was on the top and I took my time reading through it carefully, looking for anything that might be useful. It was dated October 1794 but no address had been added. Deliberate or an oversight I wondered. It read as follows.

My Dear Friend

I cannot describe the surprise and pleasure that I felt when I received your note, not from where I expected but from much closer to home. I am intrigued to hear your story but I understand your request to allow things to settle a little first. One thing that is certain is that I owe my life to you. If you hadn't carried me away from Versailles and insisted that the ships surgeon tend me, I would not be writing this now. I am happily settled here in Bordeaux and have put my old life behind me. There are multiple business opportunities here and if you ever return to France, I would seriously recommend that you consider this town. I have invested some of my profits in a share of a trading vessel that runs up and down the coast so when you feel that it is expedient to do so, I may just join them and come to visit you. Meanwhile stay safe.

Guillot

Since seeing this previously, I had examined the copy of Motte's letter and so this time I was able to piece together some pieces of information that I had overlooked before. Opening my notebook, I turned to a blank page and started to write another list.

1. Guillot had his life saved by Antoine.

2. Guillot's 'previous profession' was not an honest one.

3. He was carried away from Versailles, presumably after being wounded or injured and if the other letter was to be believed taken to Rouen.

4. A little speculation here but it would appear that Antoine had a ship waiting to take him to the American Colonies. This would make sense if he was wishing to escape France as the two countries had a treaty agreement at that time. An obvious question here then is why Antoine wished to flee France. He would not have been considered as aristocracy and so should not have been in danger because of the Revolution.

5. Guillot ended up in Bordeaux and Antoine somewhere 'closer to home' but outside France. If Guillot was to visit in a trading vessel, it would probably have an Atlantic coastline.

6. That probably meant Germany, Netherlands, Belgium, Spain or Portugal.

On the one hand, that was an awful lot of area to cover but to put a more positive spin on things, it eliminated most of the rest of the world.

The rest of the box yielded nothing of immediate relevance so

I needed to work out a strategy that might uncover more details of this man's life. I had some ideas but there was a lot of ground to cover and I couldn't do it all by myself. It was time to call in the cavalry.

15

Of course the problem with calling in the cavalry was that the workload needed to be available to be distributed amongst them and on reflection I was not ready to do that yet. There was no doubt that when required, I had all of the resources available that I could possibly need. First of all though I needed to pin down some detail instead of this needle in a haystack situation that we were currently in. There were obviously two possible starting positions and just as I was ready to make the first phone call I heard a car pull into the drive.

That's one advantage of having friends in high places, I thought, *speed limits appear not to apply.*

To have left Montignac, driven up to Versailles, collected Lillian then blasted down here to Brittany they must have been well over the speed limit for the full journey. I could hear Patrice's ebullient voice as soon as the car stopped. Of the two, he was by far and away the more gregarious, Guilbert by contrast was more reserved, more stoic but between them they made a formidable team. When they left the anti-terrorist squad several years ago, I heard that they had been in great demand as private bodyguards by some of the wealthiest people in France. Instead, both appeared to have settled down but at the slightest opportunity they would cheerfully revert to their old, more violent ways. I was just lucky that they were on my side.

A minute later I walked out through the kitchen door to see the two them, Gaston and a girl who you would not have guessed had been abducted, kept against her will and then suddenly released. Her appearance belied Gaston's description of a squalid, pierced punk who habitually wore ripped, black scruffy T-shirts. Following the shouted ' Salut Patron' greetings from Patrice and Guilbert, she turned towards me with her hand outstretched.

Behind her back Gaston raised his eyebrows mimicking shock and surprise in a single gesture. I have always been one to take people at face value and the greeting and the thanks that I received were charming. Again, without Lillian seeing him, Gaston was childishly gesturing his amazement. Trying hard to keep a straight face I welcomed her and reassured her that we would do all that was possible to help her. I was surprised when she replied that she had an idea of her own to sort out this worm, by whom I supposed that she meant Motte. When pressed she would say little else except that it would take a while to put it all together and she would need Motte to stay off her back for the duration. This suited me perfectly for as long as I was making progress Motte should stay happy. Well, as happy as a megalomaniac deluded crook could be happy.

It didn't take much to persuade Patrice and Guilbert that they had done enough driving for the day, largely I suspected, because they were keen to try out the local Breton cider. Sure enough, after asking for directions to the nearest bar, the two walked off, happy enough to leave Gaston to organise the guest sleeping arrangements.

For my own part I was keen to question both Gaston and Lillian to see if there were any clues that could be garnered from their family background. Most families had stories about their most notorious or famous relations as was obvious from Motte's rambling tales and I hoped that these two might be able to add to our knowledge of Antoine Lestrade. It wasn't really a surprise to hear that Gaston had told me everything that he knew and Lillian was unable to add anything either. Their parents were obviously not ones for family gossip and there were no surviving relatives that might have been able to help.

I knew that their apartment in Versailles had been in the family for many years and that once, they had ownership of the entire house. I had never seen it as Gaston tended to keep the details of his excursions to Paris a little secretive. It was a part of his life that he was, as far as I was concerned anyway, entitled to keep to himself. William had trusted him implicitly and in the year that he had worked for me he had been exemplary in his conduct. However, I wondered if there were any clues that I might be able to seek out, that perhaps they were so familiar with, that they had overlooked.

I asked permission to visit the place and after some discussion it was agreed that the next day, Gaston and I would pay a visit, albeit with the two cider drinkers to accompany us. I texted Patrice and warned him of the plans for the next day and received reassurance that although they were murdering the locals on the pool table, their alcohol consumption was within tolerance.

It had been another long day and I was getting hungry. On my walk earlier I had bought a kilo of mussels so it was only a matter of a few minutes to get them onto the stove, slice up some bread and open a bottle of muscadet. I knew that Gaston was a moderate drinker at best, but I soon found that Lillian had a taste for this acidic white wine and a second bottle quickly followed the first. It didn't need Gaston to repeat back to me what I had said to Patrice about the next day and in any case I had some reading to do before settling down for the night. I made my excuses and headed for the stairs. It was time for me to become more acquainted with the events of the 1790s.

It was a five hour drive to Versailles the next morning and it was noticeable that with the 'Patron' in the car, Guilbert stuck rigidly to the speed limit. Lillian had needed no persuasion to stay at my house saying that she also had work to do. The journey was uneventful and soon after we had parked the car we found ourselves being greeted by the same concierge who had needed permission to allow Lillian up to her own apartment. To his credit, he didn't so much as raise an eyebrow at Gaston despite the company of three fairly rough looking strangers. That, at least, was how I saw us when I caught a reflection in the hallway mirror. I wanted to be back in Locquirec by nightfall so there wasn't a lot of time to spare. When searching for anything like this I preferred a calm, composed atmosphere which was not possible with everybody there, so I suggested that they went off for lunch and left me to myself for a couple of hours. There was a brasserie just across the road from the apartment block entrance so they could keep an eye on anyone entering. I approached the task logically taking one room at a time and examining every bookcase, cupboard and drawer. It was fairly tedious work as I ensured that everything was put back exactly as I had found it and so the first hour passed without anything of note. At the end of the two hours I thought that I had finished with nothing to show for my efforts when I glanced for a last time around the drawing room. It had been modernised at some point in the last ten years and there was little to indicate its actual age. The windows were large, looking down onto the street below and heavy net curtains were drawn across, presumably to protect the … 'Bloody Hell.' I cursed to myself out loud then walked across to the wall opposite. Hanging in an obviously nineteenth century frame was an oil painting which showed a full length study of a man who was wearing knee length breeches, a tail coat that was cut high over those breeches, a coat with a turned up collar and a ruffled cravat. I was no expert in period clothing, but I would bet that this was typical of the end of the eighteenth, beginning of the nineteenth century. It was a matter of a few moments to lift it down from the wall and examine it more closely. The varnish was dark and grimy but it was just possible to make out a signature and a date. I wasn't familiar with the artist but a few moments with my iPhone and Google told me that Domingos Sequeira was Portuguese and the date of 1823 was absolutely right if Antoine Lestrade had returned to his home in Versailles after his travels. With perfect timing Gaston appeared and explained that he had left the other two talking to the concierge downstairs. My excitement then was tempered slightly when Gaston confessed that he had no idea who the subject of the picture was, although he did agree that it was possible that it was an heirloom handed down through the generations. It had certainly been there when he was a child.

At that point there was a quiet knock on the door and Gaston went to let them in. I was surprised to hear raised voices and even more surprised to see Gaston return from the hallway not with Patrice and Guilbert but followed by two strangers. My surprise was therefore compounded by the fact that the gentleman on the left of the two held what I surmised to be a hand gun with a long silencer on the barrel. The alarm on my face must have been obvious because Gaston pre-empted my question by saying simply. 'There is a private entrance that can't be seen from the hallway. I have no idea how these two got in that way but Patrice and Guilbert will still be downstairs.'

The man without the gun was middle aged and rounding - indeed going to fat. His clothes looked expensive, a dark wool overcoat worn with a scarf wrapped around his neck using that fastidious knot favoured by the French. When he spoke he was obviously the man in charge. His colleague was there just to make sure that we listened and as I couldn't imagine that Patrice and Guilbert would come up here for a while it was up to Gaston and myself to sort this out.

'As you may have guessed, my name is David Motte. Actually, I have just popped in to introduce myself and to check on your progress to date.'

It really was as bizarre as that. No reference to the firearm or indeed to the other man at all. No explanation of how he knew that we were in Versailles or how he had entered the building without being seen. When I heard the knock on the door I had returned the painting to its original position on the wall and as it was the first possible lead that we had, there was no way that I was going to mention it. Instead I decided to play for time.

'Monsieur Motte eh? You don't look the sort to have an ancestor as notorious as Nicholas De La Motte. If the stories are to be believed he was a real nasty piece of work and a bit of a con man as well.'

His eyes narrowed at this - I had obviously hit a raw nerve.

'My ancestor is no business of yours. Your job is simple. Find my necklace. So have you made any progress at all?'

'I really don't think you understand how this works. Historical detective work is a slow, indeed painstakingly slow and expensive process. Every fact has to be checked and rechecked; searches of documents have to be conducted - often at first hand. I don't imagine that I will have anything to report to you for some time yet as I have to wait for replies to my queries and then sift through the information that I get back.'

At this point I gathered that he was getting the message when he interrupted me saying,

'Enough. As a gentle reminder I have sent a few papers to an official that has been taking an unhealthy interest in some of my projects. The hacks that they contain are relatively minor but do lead back to your friend's sister. I doubt that they would be enough to warrant her arrest at this stage but if you show any indication of stalling, I have a lot more material that would have much more serious consequences. Find my necklace and keep me up to date with your progress.'

* * *

When I protested how unlikely it was that the necklace still existed, he simply said, 'Fine. Prove it. Now gentlemen, if you will lead the way, we are leaving the way that we arrived.'

I looked in alarm at Gaston but when a gun is waved in your direction the inclination is to follow instructions. I had noticed another door just outside the apartment entrance but as it had been locked I had paid it no real notice. It was now ajar and we were directed that way and down a stairwell. A door at the bottom led out onto the street half a block away from the main entrance. When I looked back I could even make out the shape of Patrice through the glass. I had to make a decision quickly. If I made a commotion now it was possible that passers by might take notice and even maybe attract the attention of Patrice and Guilbert. It was also possible that someone might be injured or even killed in the process. As if sensing my unease Motte spoke from behind.

'Don't be stupid. There is a silenced gun pointed at you and in any case you will be allowed to go free in a few minutes. I don't want you raising any kind of alarm that might inconvenience me.'

Sure enough, less than five minutes later, I looked over my shoulder and realised that the two had gone. I stopped in my tracks and alerted Gaston to the fact that we were now both free. A short while later Patrice and Guilbert were astonished to see us enter the vestibule from the street. With the concierge listening, I indicated for them to follow us and we returned to Gaston's apartment before speaking. The two were furious with themselves despite Gaston's protests that he was at fault for not thinking of the old private entrance.

* * *

'It was created when my family sold off the rest of the block so that they could maintain their independence. I never use it so it completely slipped my mind. How the hell they got in though, I can't imagine.'

Guilbert had stepped out to examine the doors and when he returned his gesture said it all. The locks were ancient and could have been picked by a baby.

'Give me the old keys and I will make sure that no-one ever uses this as a back door again. Apart from yourself of course.'

For Guilbert this passed as a comedy routine so we smiled obligingly and Gaston agreed to dig out the old keys.

There was little else to do here so I collected the painting once again and scrounging an old blanket I wrapped it carefully before carrying it back to the car. I was intrigued by the signature of Domingos Sequeira but I needed to get back to Locquirec to be able to follow it up properly. A quick search on my phone was fine but didn't really cut it for any extended research. In the meantime it was time for Lillian to start earning her keep. As we walked back to the car I gave her a call and instructed her to go into town. If she was going to help she needed a computer to work on. Another phone call to the shop with my card details sorted out the payment for the item so by the time we arrived back, she should be ready to start.

Sure enough, as we drove in through the gates, she was sat outside waiting for us.

* * *

'Thank you. I didn't know where you wanted me to work so I have just been playing with it down here.'

I was assuming from Gaston's description of her skills that 'playing' was just a euphemism. I outlined the task that I wanted her to do for me and suggested one of the many rooms downstairs that she could use as a workplace. I left Patrice, Guilbert and Gaston to their own devices as I was keen to find out more about the artist. I had already made the connection between the letter to Antoine Lestrade that had placed him somewhere on the Atlantic coast and the appearance of a Portuguese painter. Could it possibly be that Antoine didn't go the American Colonies but instead ended up in Portugal? It certainly seemed plausible.

Now we had several lines of enquiry. The task that I had set Lillian was to follow up on any documents that she could trace relating to shipping in Rouen in 1794. I wanted to carry out a little more research on Domingos Sequeira and last but not least, I needed someone to look at and possibly clean up the painting. Little detail could be made out through the accumulation of heavy, smoky varnish and it really needed an expert restorer to sort it out. Fortunately I knew just the person. Unfortunately, she lived in Granada in southern Spain so it looked as though Gaston was due for a trip. It was also worth trying to find out more about the author of the letter who signed himself Guillot. Lots then to be getting on with.

16

Andalucía is a beautiful part of the world in which to live and despite the fact that she had only arrived here because of the manipulations of a certain William Scott, 14th Earl of Strathearn, Shirley Holmes was happy to be residing and working in the old Moorish City of Granada. Admittedly, she had been double bluffed by the Earl when she had tried to trick him into a transaction that, had it come off, would have significantly boosted her bank balance whilst reducing his by the same amount. He had anticipated her deception and turned the tables whilst simultaneously setting her up in a studio in the old Albaicin part of town. After having helped him to unravel the story behind a mysterious painting, he had admitted that she was only trapped in Granada because of a misdirection on his part. After he died, she had been left the studio and a significant sum of money which helped towards her living expenses. Trying to make her way as an art restorer and sometimes seller of old paintings was a precarious existence at best, but then as her lover Andres would remind her, provided she was kept replete with cava and jazz her needs were simple.

As a result she was delighted to receive the telephone call from Paul. She had met him and Gaston just over a year ago whilst unraveling the mystery behind a Leonardo pastel sketch and they had remained firm friends ever since. Even so, the offer of work cleaning a picture that was en route with Gaston, was greeted with barely disguised glee. As Paul told her the full story she was surprised to hear that Gaston had a sister at all. Nonetheless, it did mean that she would be able to make her contribution to the rent on the apartment that she shared with Andres Matas Matas, lecturer in Computer Science at Granada University and fellow jazz aficionado, without eating into her savings once again. Before moving in with him she was happy sleeping on a mattress on the floor of her whitewashed studio and it took some considerable persuasion from him to move her out. When she eventually agreed she claimed that it was only because he was a worthy competitor at 'Call of Duty' on the Xbox and not because of the promise of regular sex. Andres of course, claimed that the opposite was true. Their life had slipped into an easy pattern whereby each day he rode a motor scooter up to the University campus whilst she walked down to her studio. Both acknowledged that driving a car round the narrow, traffic filled streets of Granada was not a sensible option but Shirley flatly refused to risk her neck on two wheels even as a passenger behind Andres.

It was a late flight from Nantes Atlantique Airport and Gaston had arrived early despite the fact that at this time of night there was little chance of any holdups because of traffic.

The painting was small enough to be carried onboard as hand luggage but they had ensured that it was secured in a wooden frame before wrapping it. He was sat with a small black coffee in an area that was overlooked by an enormous black and white logo proclaiming 'Café International'. *I must be getting old* he thought to himself. *I'm the only person in here that isn't wearing fluorescent trainers on my feet.* It was actually nothing to do with age, simply the fact that Gaston was fastidious in his dress and the thought of a pair of training shoes of any kind replacing his brown leather brogues was anathema to him. Eventually the flight was called and he was delighted to find that the two adjacent seats were empty.

Carefully placing his parcel under the seat in front, he stretched and closed his eyes. He had insisted that there was no need for them to meet him at the airport and just a few hours later after landing and collecting his luggage it was only a matter of minutes to find a taxi that could take him down into town. The Alhambra Palace was brightly floodlit and could easily be seen as it seemed to hover above the streets below. The apartment to which Shirley and Andres had recently moved was situated on the top floor of a building that housed a range of shops fronting onto a narrow street. Like most of this part of town it was not as old as the Moorish district, but even so it had been built several hundred years ago and of course, there was no lift up to the top floor. Fortunately, having given him entry via the video-phone system, Gaston was met half way up by an excited and ebullient Andres who took his case in one hand leaving him to negotiate the narrow bends of the staircase with just the parcel. On the landing at the top of the stairs Shirley stood with a large grin on her face. She wore a pair of old battered Levi's and a white T-shirt that boldly declared,

'A meal without wine is called breakfast.'

* * *

Before he had a chance to put down the parcel, she wrapped her arms around him and gave him a massive hug. Andres looked sideways before commenting, 'If I didn't know any better, I'd be jealous. Untangle yourself from this hussy and come on in.'

This was the first time that Gaston had seen the apartment that they shared and he had to admire the cool white interior with its floor to ceiling windows on two sides that overlooked the streets below. Looking between two buildings opposite the glories of the Alhambra Palace could be seen in the distance. A large flat screen TV was fitted to one wall and an Xbox game had obviously been paused in the middle of some action. Andres nudged Shirley to one side with his hip and instructed, 'OK woman - three glasses of Rioja if you please while I show Gaston to his room.'

Gaston couldn't help but smile at the banter between them. They were obviously very happy together, but after the events of last year which had involved the kidnapping of Shirley and an unrelated knife attack on Andres, this life must all seem quietly normal for them.

It was only a matter of a few moments to unpack his bag, hang up the tweed suit jacket that he had worn despite the climate down here in the south of Spain and make his way back to the living room. As promised, three large glasses of velvety coloured Rioja were waiting together with a selection of tapas. Shirley had already started to unwrap the parcel that he had brought and when she saw the condition of the painting, she pursed her lips in disapproval.

'My God, it is certainly showing its age. The varnish is so

dark you can't make out any of the background detail. It looks genuine enough and Sequeira isn't an artist that forgers would normally bother with. How long has it been in your family?'

Gaston took a sip of wine, thought for a moment then replied,

'I remember it being hung up when my grandparents lived there and I have always assumed that it has been in the family for ever but I cannot be certain of that. It's funny that you don't want to know about your family history until it's too late and the people that would have known have passed away.'

'It will take me a few days to clean the painting so I assume that you would prefer to wait until I have finished then take it back to Paul. It will make a massive difference and we should be able to see what has been painted in the background when it's done.'

Andres interrupted her saying loudly, 'But in the meantime we have lots to catch up on. How on earth have you kept a sister secret and what's she like? Is she as fastidious and meticulous as you?'

'Don't be so rude Andres.' Shirley interrupted with a grin then turning to Gaston she asked 'So what is she like? Tell us all.'

An hour later, a second and then a third bottle of wine had been emptied and Shirley and Andres were in turn roaring with laughter then quietly attentive as Gaston told the story of his wayward sister. Eventually, he answered a question by saying,

* * *

'No, I really haven't thought about what she will do afterwards. Go her own way as she always has I suppose. I just want to get her out of the clutches of this man David Motte. Despite his appearance he really is a nasty piece of work. Patrice and Guilbert were more than happy to sort him out but as long as he has this file on Lillian there is little they can do.'

The rest of the evening sped by and soon Gaston was taking his leave to go to bed. It had been a long and exhausting day. The next morning he was awoken by bright sunlight shining through his bedroom curtains and after a quick shower, he dressed and went in search of his hosts. There was a note waiting for him on the kitchen table explaining that the two had already left, Shirley for her studio and Andres for the University. He was instructed to help himself to breakfast so after raiding the refrigerator, he took his coffee and orange juice and went out to a spacious balcony that opened from the kitchen. It was drenched in bright sunlight and the street below was awash with sounds of traders opening up their shops and pedestrians shouting greetings to each other. This place had been carefully chosen, was his first thought, as it was high above a largely pedestrianised area and much more pleasant than if it had been overwhelmed by the constant rumbling of traffic. For the first time in a while he was able to relax a little, grateful for the fact that he now had a network of friends all willing to help his sister. He had rung Paul and Lillian the previous evening so there was little that he could do today. Perhaps it was an opportunity to be a tourist and explore some of the sites of this ancient city. While he finished his breakfast he fired up Google maps on his phone and checked the direction up to the Alhambra Palace. He was aware that there were tourist buses that had a regular route from the town centre up to the Alhambra entrance but he really felt that he would see much more on foot.

It took Shirley just two days to transform a dark, muddy oil painting into a work of light and colour that showed a cleverly detailed background. The subject of the picture was a corpulent, contented man obviously in the latter years of his life. The artist had gone to some considerable effort to show that this person was learned and well read. A book case which was on a wall to the side clearly showed the titles of a range of books and a number of pictures hung on the wall above it. She had examined the signature closely and the scrawl of Domingos Sequeira 1823 looked as genuine as she could ascertain without resorting to further scientific analysis. That could come later if Paul wanted to pursue that avenue of investigation. She emailed photographs of her work to Paul asking for further instructions. Did he want the painting back immediately or did he want her to submit it to the University for more analysis. It really depended upon what he was hoping to find. A quick phone call established that Andres was finished for the day and that he and Gaston had met up in a tapas bar down by the Darro, which at this time of year was little more than a trickle that ran in a gorge at the foot of the hill on which the Alhambra stood. A street followed the path of the gorge and the bar at which the two men had met was little more than a five minute walk from Shirley's studio. With dire threats as to what would happen if there wasn't a glass of sparkling cava waiting for her, she locked up, entered the alarm code and set out in the late afternoon sunshine. She had definitely been conned into living here in the first place but it was exactly what she would have chosen if choice had come into it at all. Additionally, there was the bonus of having met the deliciously good looking Dr. Andres Matas Matas. When he first told her his name she thought that he had stuttered with nerves, but he patiently explained that the tradition in Spain was to take the surnames of both your mother and father. By coincidence rather than breeding, both of his parents had the same surname - hence Matas Matas. 'Like New York, I was so good they named me twice.'

It was a glorious place to eat and drink and they were in no hurry to move on. Apart from the previous evening it was the first time since they had originally met that they had a chance to talk and with the alcohol lubricating the conversation, topics ranged from the couple themselves; 'Any plans to marry yet?' asked Gaston cheekily although he noticed that they pointedly avoided an answer, through to Paul's girlfriends and even a question about romance in Gaston's life. The reply was a slightly melancholic, 'Sadly the right man hasn't come along yet.'

It was at this point that they were interrupted by the ringtone of Shirley's mobile phone. She glanced at the caller ID and said to the others, 'It's Paul. Sober voices please.' Just as she pressed it to answer, Gaston and Andres glanced at each other and burst out into a fit of laughter. They could only hear her end of the conversation but it was obvious that Paul was in a more sombre mood than they were. They heard Shirley reassure him that they were not leading Gaston down the path of debauchery and yes she was sober enough to do it - whatever 'it' was. With a cheery goodbye she turned to them to explain. 'He thinks that he's found something on the painting but he needs some close up photographs of parts of the background. Party's over boys - it's back to work I'm afraid.'

There was the usual mock fight over who was paying the bill

which Gaston won by calling for house guest privileges. 'OK - but it's our turn when we come to France next time' Andres replied.

Retracing Shirley's earlier passage they soon found themselves in a whitewashed alley with a large green industrial looking door facing on to the street. It was opened by an eight digit code which Shirley entered onto a keypad.

'It always surprises me that it hasn't been vandalised but even the local streets are graffiti free. It certainly wouldn't happen in London.'

Once inside the door she entered another code into the alarm system and they walked up a staircase to the main part of the studio. The painting was on a tall wooden easel to one side of a table that held a range of solvents, pads and brushes. It was the first time that the two men had seen this cleaned up version and both were astonished at the transformation.

'So this is possibly one of your ancestors?' asked Andres.

'If Paul's guesswork is correct, then his name is Antoine Lestrade and he lived in Versailles in the late eighteenth and early nineteenth centuries. I must say that I don't see any family resemblance but then I suppose I wouldn't expect to. I didn't even look anything like either of my parents.'

Shirley added her opinion

'His clothing is about right for that time period and the signature and date at the bottom of the painting are genuine as far as I can tell without further analysis. The fact that it's been in your family home for some time is probably indicative as well. Paul may well be right.'

She went across to a desk which was carefully placed by the far wall and took a digital SLR Nikon out of one of the drawers. Checking that it had a memory card in the slot she screwed it to a tripod that she had placed in front of the picture and using the zoom lens carefully focused on a number of areas, taking several photographs of each.

'I may have been a little over enthusiastic last time,' she admitted. 'I just shot a photograph with my iPhone and sent that. Paul obviously needs more detail.'

She extracted the memory card and slotted it into her iMac. A few minutes later and the latest pictures were attached to an email and were on their way to the north coast of Brittany.

'OK. Unless he wants even more detail I think that we have definitely finished here. I suggest that more cava is the order of the day. With that she led the way back out and carefully locking up set a path to another tapas bar that she and Andres had waxed lyrical about.

It was getting late and they had switched their drink from sparkling wine to a local hot chocolate speciality when her phone pinged. This time it was a text message, again from Paul. It read simply.

'Too late to talk now. However, start to pack your bags as I have a trip that I would like you to take. Usual rates and all expenses paid. I'll ring tomorrow'

'I like the sound of all expenses paid. Paul doesn't realise how I can interpret this description!'

Converging Lines

17

An airport arrivals area is no place to meet someone, particularly if they are a total stranger, Shirley was thinking as she manipulated her carry on luggage through the crowds. Following Paul's instructions she had flown from Granada to Lisbon packing for a trip of just a few days. The problem was, that although fluent in French and Spanish, her knowledge of Portuguese was pretty non-existent and trying to carry out the research that Paul had demanded was going to be close to impossible. She knew exactly where to start and how to follow up leads, but being unable to hold a conversation or read a document put her at a major disadvantage. Paul's first suggestion was that she hire a translator, but he was interrupted in mid conversation and with an apology had put his iPhone on hold for a few minutes while he continued the conversation with someone else. When he re-established the connection he had said,

* * *

'New plan. It seems that Lillian can speak Portuguese pretty well because of her work so I'll send her to join you in Lisbon. We might as well keep everything 'in house' if we can.'

And so Shirley found herself looking for a girl of a similar age based on a description given by Paul that pretty much matched half of the women that were walking by.

Typical male, she thought after stopping a third passenger and being assured that, no - she wasn't called Lillian.

Suddenly her mobile phone buzzed and when she answered it Lillian herself spoke, saying, 'Hi Shirley, I'm sat at the bar at the end of the arrivals area with two large glasses of wine. Paul's description of you was useless so I gave up looking. I promise not to drink yours provided you are here within the next five minutes.'

Two minutes later Shirley sat down opposite a girl who she could only describe as 'striking'. Neither Paul's nor Gaston's descriptions had come close to accurately describing the ex Goth who was grinning across at her. She was dressed simply in jeans and black T-shirt but her cheek bones were pronounced and her black hair was cut in a modern razor bob that really suited her. An hour later the two were still sat talking as if they had known each other for years. Lillian had found someone to whom she could explain how her life had unravelled over the last few years and Shirley in turn was a good listener. When she was asked about her knowledge of the Portuguese language her reply was tinged with regret.

'When I was working for Motte, I specialised in writing malware that was targeted at wealthy Brazilians. It was a new market and they were wide open. He must have eventually made a fortune out of the more gullible but when it was being planned none of the team spoke Portuguese so I was tasked with learning the language in order to set up the front end apps. Somehow I took to it like, I suppose, a fish to water. When I overheard Paul's conversation with you I offered to take the place of his suggestion of an interpreter. It seemed that it was the least I could do to help. So tell me about the painting that you cleaned. There seemed to be something about it that had Paul quite excited.'

While Shirley swiped through the photos on her phone to show Lillian what she was talking about, she explained.

'In order to follow the path of this necklace, if it still exists, it seems that the events of Antoine Lestrade and Nicholas De La Motte in the 1790's and early 1800's are critical. Paul is a genius at tracking down historical artefacts but the hardest part is always starting out. He recognised that the artist was a Portuguese portrait painter and by putting two and two together he surmised that Antoine had left France for Portugal rather than the new Colonies as Motte assumes. If Antoine knew of the whereabouts of this necklace there may be documentation buried in an archive somewhere. We just have to follow his trail and find it. It seems that we have got the Portuguese end of the trail while Paul follows it through France. Personally, I doubt that the thing still exists but if we are seen to be making an effort, it will keep Motte off your back while Paul thinks of something.'

'I'm not sure that Paul is going to be able to solve that little problem but I have some ideas of my own. It's just going to take some time to put them together. Anyway, maybe it's time to make our way into town. If you know where we are staying the taxi rank is that way.'

It was only a twenty minute ride down to Rossio Square where they were booked into a pleasant, modern hotel and after agreeing to meet up later they went their separate ways.

After unpacking her case, Shirley opened up her laptop and found several emails waiting for her. There was the usual rubbish but sent just an hour ago was a long message from Paul. When she had spoken to him the day before he hadn't given any detail about what he had seen on the picture that had so excited him, but the email was full of information. In particular, there was a bookcase behind the subject and the titles of the books could clearly be seen. After some extensive work Paul had narrowed down two that were particularly interesting. The first was titled Crata Repoa, a book which described a Rosicrucian initiation ceremony. The Rosicrucians were a society that flourished in the eighteenth century and what was particularly exciting was that one of their leading members was a man known as the Baron da Regaleira who owned an estate near to Sintra, a town just forty kilometres from Lisbon. He had been here in 1794 when, if Paul's conjectures were correct, Antoine had landed and lived in this area. The other book that seemed to support this was a novel with the title of 'Vathek' which had been written by an English gentleman called William Beckford. Having read this far, Shirley wasn't surprised to see that Beckford was also living close to Sintra. It wouldn't be an enormous stretch of the imagination to connect Antoine Lestrade with both of these people.

It was a little later when the two women met up again and after deciding to find a nearby pastelaria, they sat with coffee and one of the delicious custard tarts that these café's were named after.

'So our starting point is here in Lisbon first then we will need to visit Sintra to see what we can find there. Paul is using his credentials as a 'famous historian' to contact various people on our behalf to make introductions '

'Presumably he will disguise the real reason for our research here?' asked Lillian to which Shirley replied simply, 'Yes. We are helping to research some material for his next book on the French Revolution and its impact on Portugal. That will give us enough scope and flexibility to ask any questions that we think are relevant to our specific interests.'

As the two continued to discuss the practicalities of the work that faced them the street lights started to turn on until eventually Lillian said, 'I think that I'm turning in for an early night. Instead of the hotel breakfast, I've read about a brilliant coffee shop that is just five minutes from here. It's got great reviews and a Portuguese breakfast to die for.'

'OK. I want to ring Andres and bring him up to date. You must come out to Granada soon. You and he have such a lot in common. I'll see you at 'Fabri' at nine o'clock in the morning.'

Five minutes later she was talking quietly as Andres listened intently. He wasn't surprised that Paul had already made inroads into the problem nor that he had two young attractive women doing the legwork for him.

'Come on Andres. He's just using the best available people for the job. And I get paid well. And I get to come to Lisbon. And I'll get to see Sintra.'

* * *

'Just you take care then. The last time you did any work for him you ended up getting kidnapped.'

After saying goodnight Shirley ordered another coffee and looked longingly at the counter. 'One more of those custard tarts as well please.'

At nine o'clock the next morning Shirley pushed open the door of Fabri coffee shop and smiled at the way that it had been set out. For a start she could see a copy of a medieval panel hanging on an industrial brick wall. The fans on the ceiling were made from old ships propellers and the furniture was an eclectic mix of what seemed to be have been recycled from a nearby skip. She loved it. Reggae music was blasting out through what sounded like an advanced sound system and looking round she noticed that several MacBooks had already made an appearance as the coffee shop workforce focused on coding and cappuccino.

Lillian was sat on an old, battered, comfortable looking leather sofa with a table in front of her.

Ordering her favourite macchiato, Shirley sat down and commented, 'How do you manage to eat a breakfast like that and stay as thin as a latt? If I even looked at it I would put on pounds.'

Wiping the crumbs from her mouth Lillian simply replied, 'Nervous energy I guess. So what's the plan for today?'

'After breakfast, we have a meeting at the Gulbenkian museum. It's about a half hour walk from here so it will give me chance to burn off a few calories. I'm afraid that the rest of the day will be spent scouring their archives for anything that we think might be relevant. It may take us a few days to cover the material that has been stored for the time period that we are interested in. After that, there is something that we need to follow up in a town called Sintra that is a short train ride from Lisbon.'

The next half hour was taken up with an intense concentration focused on the range of coffees, juices and breakfast treats that were available. Eventually they made their way out of the door and crossing the backstreet, turned up a wide tree lined boulevard which was packed with designer label shops. This slowed them down significantly and it was just at the time of the arranged meeting that they entered the large, concrete and marble vestibule of the Calouste Gulbenkian Foundation. As well as a modern art gallery and exhibition space there was a large concert hall and of more specific interest to them, a research centre and extensive archive. A jovial middle aged man greeted them warmly as protégés of Señor Paul and after giving them both employee passes walked with them to a wing of the building to which the public were excluded. After showing them the records for the time period in which they were interested he bid them farewell and left them to their own devices. Dismayed by the rows and rows of document files Lillian turned to Shirley with an exclamation of panic. 'We can try our best but this looks like an impossible task.'

'As Yoda said, there is only do or don't do. There is no try!! My favourite quote from Star Wars. It's simple. We start at 1794 and glance through the papers looking for references to Antoine Lestrade, William Beckford, Nicholas De La Motte, the artist Domingos Sequeira or Baron da Regaleira. Beckford and the Baron are really outside shots but who knows. There's a coffee machine in the corridor so my round first then we get started.'

When Shirley came back a few minutes later with two steaming plastic cups Lillian had already taken down the first file and had started to turn page after page as she skim read through each one.

'It's a pity they haven't digitised their collection. It would have made this so much easier. Maybe we offer to take it on as a project when all of this is finished.'

Two days later they had left Fabri after another eclectic breakfast and were making their way up the hill past all of the shop windows. Suddenly, Lillian pulled Shirley to look at a shoulder bag but as they stepped towards the shop she said in a low voice, 'Check the reflection of the man that is about to walk past.' They stood still for several minutes but when no one appeared Lillian looked over her shoulder and muttered, 'He's gone.'

'Who has gone?' asked Shirley with bewilderment in her voice.

'Tall, gelled grey hair, red glasses. He's been in Fabri's every morning.'

'So what? There have been a number of people in there. He's probably a local.'

'Maybe, but he was also in the café at the museum when we were having lunch yesterday. And I thought that he seemed to be particularly interested in our conversation at the time.'

* * *

'Well he's not here now but I'll watch out for him. Probably just someone who fancies you.'

Later that day Shirley decided to ring Paul with an update. It had been particularly interesting as, after trawling through hundreds of documents, they had finally started to make progress. She tried to keep the excitement out of her voice in an attempt to maintain a professional demeanour. Giving up on that she simply blurted out, 'We've found something. You were right with your guesses. Back in 1794, it seems that both William Beckford and the Baron da Regaleira were living in Sintra just a couple of miles from each other. We have the rental and purchase agreements that they took out at the time in front of us now. It is too much of a coincidence to assume that Antoine Lestrade wasn't somehow connected with them, perhaps even visiting them there. Can you contact the estate owners and arrange access for us. There must be a ton of stuff buried away there that we need to look at.

By the end of the day, Shirley declared that they had extracted everything relevant from the archive.

'If Paul gets his finger out with his contacts we are heading for Sintra tomorrow. Let's see if we can narrow down Antoine's stay there. We're close to something - I feel it. The trouble is, I'm not sure what. Come on - let's head back and grab one of those custard tarts on the way.'

Stopping off to thank the archivist who had originally met them took some time and it was starting to get dark as they walked out of the entrance hall. Turning left they started down the hill and as usual turned to take the short cut across the large central park. The benches were normally populated with young couples or local dropouts but tonight it was strangely quiet. As they followed the path around a large clump of bushes two men suddenly stepped out. They were similarly dressed in long, dark woollen overcoats with scarves around their necks. In the weak light cast by the overhead lamps they looked dark and menacing, a shadow was thrown across their faces. 'Deliberate?' wondered Shirley. They stepped to go around them but the taller of the two simply stepped sideways. Then, suddenly, Lillian took one step forward and lashed out with her foot, stamping hard just below his knee. He fell to the floor with a scream that suggested that all was not well. As Shirley looked on in admiration and amazement Lillian turned towards the one left standing and this time she had whipped a can of pepper spray out of her bag and was pointing it threateningly at the man. At this point he put up his hands in a placatory manner.

'I only wanted to talk. I apologise if this oaf frightened you although I suspect that he now regrets that.'

'OK so talk. First of all who the hell are you?'

Before he had a chance to reply Lillian intervened saying, 'This is the man I told you about this morning, he's been following us around. I think that I'm just going to pepper spray him for the hell of it.'

Looking alarmed, he spoke quickly. 'My name isn't important but I have a request. Please, give up your search and don't go to Sintra tomorrow. Yes, I know what you are looking for and I know where you are going. I have friends in the Gulbenkian and you weren't exactly discrete with your conversations.'

* * *

'Not a cat in hells chance. We are going to Sintra and as you have seen, we are fully capable of looking after ourselves.'

Without waiting to hear his reply, Shirley stepped past him and walked quickly away. Lillian looked for a moment as though she was going to use the canister but instead turned and caught up with her friend.

They reached the exit from the park a few minutes later and spotting a brightly lit bar they pushed their way through the door and ordered two drinks. Once sat at a table Lillian turned to Shirley who hadn't spoken a word in the last few minutes and said, 'We should have questioned him further. He might have told us more about this business.'

Shirley was shaking. 'I'm sorry but I am furious and I wasn't thinking. I am sick and tired of people assuming that they can use us to get their own way. Last year I was taken and held. This year it was you. Who do these people think they are? But you're right. We might have got more out of him although I suspect that he'd said as much as he was going to. Just do me a favour though and don't tell anyone about what just happened. Not yet anyway. I know for a fact that both Paul and Andres will want us to give up and go back if they think that there is any danger involved. Like I said, I'm sick of being the victim. That kick that you delivered was the best thing that I've ever seen. The sound that he made was brilliant.'

'Finish your wine. I want another and it's my round. I completely agree and I know for a fact that Gaston would go all protective big brother on me as well. There's a mystery to solve here and we are the ones who are going to solve it.'

18

The walk from the railway station to the hotel in Sintra took much longer than it should have done. First of all there were the tourists packing the main road through the town. Shirley didn't help when she insisted on stopping every few yards to admire a view of the hills or to look at the architecture of the old Palace. Finally, Lillian decided that enough was enough and sat down abruptly at an empty outside table at a café that allowed Shirley to stare at the medieval royal residence whilst she ordered refreshments. After just a few days the two had become such firm friends that there was no need for her to ask whether it was too early for wine. She had seen the latest in a long line of T-shirts that Shirley favoured, this one declaring, 'With wine and hope, anything is possible.'

By the time they had finished their glass the crowds had thinned slightly and it was only a few more minutes before they were checking in at the reception desk. They had been late in setting off so by the time they had unpacked, there was just time for dinner before settling down for an early night.

The following morning Shirley made some enquiries at the hotel reception desk and decided that they would make their way up to Beckford's estate of Monserrate Palace using the local bus. She was put off the thought of hiring a car and driving by the description of steep narrow roads often filled with tourist traffic. Paul had worked his magic again and managed to get them an introduction to the current owner of the estate who it seemed was a relative of William Beckford who had rented the place in 1794 when, as they now suspected, Antoine Lestrade might have stayed as a guest. She had telephoned to check that the new owner would be there and was happy for them to visit and was pleased when his wife, who had answered, suggested that they bring an overnight bag to save the tortuous journey back into town at the end of the day. The bus was busy with visitors to the area but they were fortunate enough to obtain the last two seats as the changes in speed and direction as the bus climbed out of town made it an uncomfortable ride for those who had been forced to stand. Eventually, they were dropped off at a stop and following the directions that they had been given, set off to walk the few hundred yards to the main entrance. The large wrought iron gates were closed with no obvious method of entry but as they stopped and looked around, Lillian pointed to an entry phone mounted on the wall.

'He obviously likes his privacy,' she commented and then waited for Shirley to push the button and listen for a reply. An accented woman's voice distorted by static welcomed them and as it was directing them to wait just inside the gate swung open. A few moments after they walked through the gate swung closed again leading Lillian to remark, 'Sensors and a timer. Simple but effective.'

It was a hot day and the walk from the bus stop had been uncomfortable. A large eucalyptus tree cast enough shade for them to stand and cool down for the few minutes that it took the owner to drive up from the house. A Mercedes SUV suggested that their host was not short of money but the driver that emerged was not quite what they were expecting. A tall elegant lady dressed in an expensive looking floral summer dress stepped out and took each of their hands.

'Welcome to Monserrate Palace. I am Gina. My husband Ian gives his apologies but he had to leave to deal with some urgent business problem that has arisen this morning. No matter. You will meet him in due course but in the meantime you will have full access to the library and family documents that we have. He tells me that you are researchers for the famous historian Mr. Paul Breslin.'

Thanking her for giving them access, Shirley climbed into the front seat whilst continuing the conversation leaving Lillian to sit in the back. Only half listening as they drove through the parkland Lillian was lost in her own thoughts. It was easy to believe that she was retracing the footsteps of her ancestor and it looked as though this landscape might not have changed a great deal during the intervening years. The drive to the palatial house swept past a large lake with a bridge at one end and a waterfall tumbling down a cliff face. As soon as they pulled up in front of a large imposing door Gina jumped out and offering tea and coffee after their journey, directed them to the guest rooms in order to 'freshen up'. After dropping off their bags they made their way down to the drawing room where a silver tray with coffee and tea was waiting. The room was large with chalky red coloured walls and furnished by antiques that looked to be several hundred years old.

Gina was sat waiting for them and explained that her husband had re-furnished and decorated the house in a manner that was as close to the descriptions that they had of it in its prime.

'We have a room full of document files that the Beckford's have accumulated over the years. Every bill, every purchase, it's all recorded. Who knows, there may be something there that will help your research. We also have a library with some of the books going back to the eighteenth century. You are welcome to stay as long as you wish. Our staff will look after you. Ian will be back tomorrow and I can usually be found out and about in the grounds.'

The view from the windows were stunning and Lillian watched a rabbit run down the lawn towards the lake. She was startled by the muffled sound of a gunshot as the rabbit dropped dead in its tracks.

'It's a shame but they are ruining the lawn. Our estate manager José and Ian are having some sort of competition as to who can collect the most scalps.'

The rest of the day was taken up with a tour of the house and grounds. Gina was a generous hostess and by the time they had returned to the drawing room she simply said, 'Minha casa é sua casa - my house is your house, but now I have things to do. Please excuse me but we will meet for dinner at 8.00 on the terrace.'

After she had left Lillian turned to Shirley saying, 'I don't know about you but I could get used to this.'

Shirley however was already walking out of the room and down the corridor towards the library. It was a sumptuous room with ceiling high bookcases all around. She stepped inside with Lillian following in her wake. Without pausing she went to the far wall and carefully took out a book that she had recognised earlier on the tour.

'Look. It's a novel by Voltaire in pristine condition and I suspect that it's a first edition. It must be worth a fortune. It might even have been here when Antoine visited.'

She sat down in a leather chair to examine it more closely, but after a few minutes realised that Lillian was waiting patiently.

'OK. I think today can be explore and get our bearings time but tomorrow it is seriously down to work. I have a good feeling about this place.'

As they walked through the double doors onto the terrace, Lillian turned towards Shirley and said, 'Do you mind me asking a personal question?'

'Go ahead. If I don't like it I won't answer, but there is very little in my life that is secret.'

'I know that you moved to Granada because of Paul's mentor William Scott but I get the impression that there was some sort of coercion. What actually happened?'

Shirley looked a little abashed as she paused for a moment then started to speak.

* * *

'It wasn't my finest hour but in the end it worked out beautifully. It started when I left university and went to work for Christie's auction house in New York. I was there for two years but when I returned to Britain I couldn't find a job. I had a stupid idea that I could scam William by selling him a fake painting. He was much smarter than I realised and when he noticed, instead of handing me in to the police, he made up a story that they were looking for me, but if I would do some work for him in Spain he would set me up in a studio there. He then cleverly fed me the line that if I left Spain I would be arrested. That was the stick. The carrot was that he kept me in work finding and restoring old paintings for him. It was lucrative work for me but it made him a small fortune. It was only when I met Paul for the first time and this business last year came to a head that he told me the truth, that in fact he had been conning me. I was furious at first but quickly realised that I was actually living a life that I had always dreamed of. I made loads of friends including Andres who I'm now living with. When William died he left me the studio in his will, so I am pretty well set up and also Paul occasionally sends work my way. That's it really. I made a stupid choice but I was really lucky how things worked out for me.'

'Yeah. We all make stupid decisions. Looking back I can't believe how naive and stupid I was. Because of me, Gaston and through him Paul, are being held to ransom by this obnoxious criminal David Motte.'

Shirley smiled.

'Believe me, Paul Breslin is way too smart and has too many contacts to allow anyone to manipulate him. He will have his own agenda in this game. Paul will have an angle on this and if getting you out of the mess is a result as well, then so much the better.'

As they talked they walked down across the grass until they stood on the edge of the large lake. Turning left they followed the edge until the lawn gave way to a rocky outcrop. There was a path winding upwards that they followed until it gave way to a bridge crossing a stream which tumbled down onto a waterfall. It was a glorious place and Lillian promised herself that she would make the most of it while she had the chance. She had spent all of her life in either Versailles or Paris and was unaccustomed to this feeling of space that she was experiencing now. Typically, as a local, she had rarely visited the gardens of the Versailles Palace and even when she had it had been during holiday time and therefore full of tourists. The space and solitude here were glorious. Eventually, somewhat reluctantly, they retraced their steps and started back towards the house. They were half way across the lawn when Lillian stopped suddenly and grabbed Shirley's arm. Pointing at the window on the first floor she spoke in an alarmed voice. 'Up there in the window above the archway. I saw a face and I'm certain that it's the man who stopped us in the park yesterday.'

Seeing nothing Shirley asked, 'Are you sure. There's no-one there now and it is very shady up there.'

'No, I'm not certain. Maybe yesterday shook me up more than I thought. There definitely was a face there for a moment, but I could easily have been mistaken about its identity. Look, I think that maybe we ought to make a start today. There is a lot of material to get through and the sooner we start, the sooner we finish.'

* * *

Shirley thought it a little strange that Lillian was suddenly in so much of a hurry but she said nothing other than to agree. Together they went into the library again and after agreeing to look for traces of Antoine Lestrade here first, they would leave the file room for the following day.

They had already decided that they would target any copies of the two books, that could be seen in the background of the portrait of Antoine, that Paul had focused upon. Additionally, anything written in French that they could date to around 1794 might be relevant as well. It was easy but tedious work discarding shelf after shelf but eventually after an hour or so, Shirley muttered, 'Got you' and pulled out a beautifully bound, leather covered tome and carefully carried it to the table in the centre of the room. On the spine and front cover written in gold coloured gothic script was the title 'Vathek' and underneath it the name of the author William Beckford.

'It could just be a coincidence but the book is pretty obscure and even back then I'm guessing that it didn't sell many copies. Of course, the fact that the author lived here for a while might be the only reason that it's here. The fact that Antoine felt it important enough to highlight in his picture must surely be relevant. Ok, that's one down. Let's keep looking.'

By the time that they needed to start getting ready for dinner with their hostess they had looked at about half of the books in the room. The biggest problem was, that to their annoyance, there was no system at all with the placement of the books on the shelves that they could see. Modern biographies were located next to pamphlets that were hundreds of years old and so it was necessary to examine every item in turn.

'I don't know about you but I have a feeling that we're going to be a little underdressed for tonight's meal. Gina Beckford seems to be quite an elegant lady. Never mind, we don't have a choice and even on a good day there's no chance of me competing with her.'

Shirley smiled to herself after hearing this from her friend. From all that she knew of Lillian, just a week ago she would probably not have been allowed through the gates. There were some advantages of de-punking but she didn't allow herself to say anything.

An hour later they declared themselves ready to face the world. They were dressed similarly in Jeans and T-shirts with little makeup. As usual Shirley carried her message of the day to the world for all to see. This time it was a quotation from Pliny the elder. It read

'In wine there's truth.'

Lillian, in keeping with her attempt to clean up her appearance, was wearing a simple white T-shirt. They made their way from the guest wing to the drawing room where Gina Beckford stood by the window with a drink in her hand. Contrary to their expectations she had simply exchanged the summer dress that she had been wearing earlier for a simple and plain coloured blouse and matching skirt. There was no sign of jewellery at all except for the wedding ring on her finger. As before, she was friendly and welcoming and insisted that they poured themselves a drink before listening to details of their progress.

* * *

'I can imagine your frustration at the lack of organisation in the library. David's ancestor William Beckford, originally rented this place, but loving it so much eventually bought it for a pittance. The problem is that there have been frequent guests over the years and as there has never been, to my knowledge, a system anyway it has simply become more chaotic as people borrow and return books.'

Dinner was a simple affair with grilled fish and salad and the three women found it easy to talk, comparing life in Portugal, Spain and France. They stuck to the story about carrying out the research for Paul, mischievously describing him as an eccentric reclusive. Eventually Gina apologised, but explained that she was tired and was going to go to bed. She insisted that Lillian and Shirley finish their drinks at least before retiring and bidding them goodnight she left the room.

The next morning the two continued the conversation that had been started the night before.

'Whatever you do don't tell Paul that we said that he was eccentric.'

'Not a chance, but what is he really like. I only met him for a few hours when I was released in Paris but he seemed like a really nice guy.'

'He is but don't let that fool you. He can be quite driven when he wants to be and he's got a really sharp brain. He realises that he's in a very fortunate position but he doesn't take advantage of it and he can be really generous. He puts a lot of work my way and although he can make a fair amount of money out of finding lost paintings he pays me well to restore them and carry out some of his research. Having said that, work has been quiet lately so I was really glad when he telephoned with this job.'

'What about Andres? Don't you miss being away from him?'

'Of course, but he has a heavy workload at the University, and to be honest I do like getting away for a while at least.'

Shirley stopped speaking as she heard footsteps on the wooden floor of the corridor and looked as the large oak door of the drawing room was pushed open. A tall man with gelled grey hair and red spectacles wearing an expensive charcoal grey suit stood in front of them. They had met him a few days before when he had stopped them as they crossed the park on the way back from the Gulbenkian Museum. He had warned them against coming to Sintra and now he was here glowering down at them.

19

'I told you I'd seen his face in the window,' was the only thing that Lillian could think of to say.

'And I told you not to come here,' he growled in reply. 'I suppose that I need to introduce myself. My name is Ian Beckford and my family have owned Monserrate Palace since the 1790s'. You have already met my wife Gina, but it is I that spoke with Paul Breslin and agreed to your visit.'

Not waiting for him to continue, Shirley interrupted asking the obvious question, 'But just yesterday you warned us off coming here. Can you not make up your mind?'

'It is a long and complex story, but for the moment it is sufficient to say that circumstances changed between me agreeing to your visit and then our meeting. Yes - they changed quite radically. I will tell the full story in due course, but in the meantime I want you to know that I will give you all the help that I can in your pursuit of the so called Queen's necklace. Yes you see, I know the real reason for your visit here and I will do all that I can to help you. However, as you are aware there are others that are less obliging and it is important that you stay out of their control. I refer, of course, to David Motte and his group of thugs. Please continue to enjoy my hospitality whilst you continue your search. I have a feeling that you will find the information that you seek here in Sintra'

With that he suddenly turned away and walked rapidly out of the door.

'My God that was strange. Yesterday, you missed the chance to question him in Lisbon and today he tells us half a story then walks off.'

'I have a feeling that it is much less than half the story. Anyway, you heard him - he says he will tell us 'in due course' whatever that means but in the meantime we have work to do.

The search through the remainder of the library threw up two gems. First of all, Lillian was on the verge of declaring a lunch break when she pounced on one of the highest shelves in the room.

'Wasn't the 'Crata Repoa' one of the books that Paul found in the background of the painting? There is a copy here and again, looking at the dust on the top, I would guess it's not been touched for ages.'

Carefully placing it on the table she opened the cover and

immediately stopped whilst trying to decipher the spidery handwriting on the title page.

'It's a name and I am pretty sure that it says William Beckford. I think that we're getting somewhere. The trouble is, I'm not sure where somewhere is.'

'No. When you think about it all we have established so far is that two of the books in the painting, the two that Paul thinks are relevant, are here in the library. There isn't yet a connection to Antoine and even if we could prove that he had been here, there isn't likely to be anything that allows us to continue the trail.'

'Except this!!'

While Shirley had been talking, Lillian had been carefully thumbing through the book and she was in the process of pulling out a sheet of paper.

'Look at this. It's a set of notes written in French, translating sections of the book with extra comments added for good measure. For example there is a long paragraph here about an initiation ceremony with a page and paragraph reference. Immediately afterwards it says 'The initiation Well at the Quinta da Regaleira' and it gives a date. October 14th 1796.'

'It's a long shot but what if this was written by Antoine. The date fits in, but of course it could have been produced by any visitor at the time.'

'Hang on. Didn't you say that Paul had a copy of a letter that was written by Antoine to a friend. Surely it must be possible to compare the handwriting. Perhaps we need to get this to him immediately while we continue looking. You need to photograph it before we mention it to our host. I don't trust him at all and it is his property. Then we need to continue searching. There may be more tucked away.'

'Unfortunately it was the other way round. The letter was written by a friend of Antoine's called Guillot and sent to him. Pity about that.'

The day passed slowly with no further success. That evening, the two of them found that both Ian and Gina were waiting for them in the drawing room. Wasting no time, Ian offered them a drink then enquired as to their progress.

'Before going in to that I think that you need to explain what your connection to Motte is and why you changed your mind about allowing us access here. Also, why you went to that trouble to try to frighten us off rather than just saying no.'

'I'll come to Motte in due course but isn't it obvious why I changed my mind. I fear that you have underestimated the reach that Motte has and how dangerous he can be. I was concerned that if you continued with this search it would end badly for you. At first I agreed to Mr Breslin's request because your goals are complementary with my own. However, when I heard that Motte had followed you to Lisbon, I determined that it had become too dangerous and that you would be far better giving up this search. You do realise that even if you find this artefact he would then, at best, continue to manipulate you and anyone connected to you.'

There was silence for a moment whilst they absorbed what he had just said.

* * *

'One thing at a time. He couldn't have followed us to Lisbon. First of all he never leaves Paris and secondly, there is no way that he could have known where we were going.'

'Wrong on both counts I'm afraid. He does leave Paris, rarely admittedly, but when the occasion warrants it he has been known to travel. As for following you, it couldn't have been simpler. There are a limited number of airports from which you can travel in your part of France and a small amount of money goes a long way when bribing officials to watch out for you.'

'So why change your mind? First of all you agree to us coming here then instead of saying no, you try to frighten us off.'

'Wrong again I'm afraid. If you recall I said that I wanted to talk to you. I was actually going to tell you what I have just told you now and ask you to be more careful. Instead, my friend was lucky to escape with nothing more than a seriously bruised shin. You are a very impetuous lady.'

'But what is your connection with Motte? You obviously know him well but you are warning us off him. I don't understand at all.'

Gina, who had sat silently during this exchange, spoke quietly for the first time.

'And thereby lies a tale. I would suggest that we eat first and then I promise that I will tell you everything that you need to know. It's a long story going back several hundred years.'

* * *

Shirley looked at Lillian then agreed saying, 'I will hold you to your promise.'

Once again dinner was a simple affair of lamb chops and salad and the two women were plied with questions about their background, how they came to be working for Paul and particularly how Lillian had become entangled with Motte in the first place.

'And so,' she concluded, 'he ultimately holds my future in his hands. If a copy of this file reaches the authorities I will be locked up for many years. Not surprisingly I am not keen on the idea.'

'I will warn you again. He is capable of much worse. You need to be very careful where he is concerned. He is a man to stay away from.'

With that warning ringing in their ears they were led by Gina back into the drawing room where the evening had started out. Ian took some time making sure that everyone was comfortable and had drinks by their side before saying, 'I'm going to let Gina tell this story. It belongs to her as much as it does to me or to anyone else for that matter'

She started by asking a question.

'What do you know about the Rosicrucians?'

This caught them by surprise and it was a few moments before Shirley replied. 'Some sort of secret society? Links with the Masons? I thought though, that they were a fictitious group made up by some author.'

* * *

'They are certainly a group of like minded people but they despise the suggestion of a secret society. Their origins are not really clear but back in the 18th century they were connected with the Royal Society who had their headquarters in London. Presidents of the Royal Society at that time included people such as Isaac Newton and Christopher Wren so you can imagine that their background was solid. Members of the Royal Society were largely philanthropic, devoting time and money to charitable causes and many, wishing to keep this side of their life private, became members of the group known as the Rosicrucians who despite their protestations tended to hide their activities from general gaze. As well as the connection with charitable work, the two groups had much in common in terms of scientific discovery so it was no surprise that there was a great deal of overlapping membership. Eventually, some members of the Rosicrucians took a different, divergent path. Their interest was in alchemy and the pursuit of arcane knowledge and they disdained the thought of devoting time and energy to charitable work. They believed literally in the original dogma and even produced a pamphlet that they called 'Pacts with the Devil' attesting that this was the path to true knowledge. And so two groups of people with radically differing philosophies took ownership of the name 'Rosicrucian'. Both groups still exist today. Motte belongs to one of these branches, Ian and I to the other. Mr. Breslin probably isn't aware of it but his mentor William Scott was also a member of our group. His death was a great tragedy and he will be seriously missed.'

There was a silence that lasted for several minutes before Shirley spoke in an incredulous voice.

'William Scott, 14th Earl of Strathearn was a member of the

Rosicrucian Society?'

'Yes, but a member of our group. The one that we believe to be the true brotherhood. I hope that improves our credentials in your eyes. However, I cannot emphasise enough the evil that permeates the offshoot that Motte belongs to.'

The conversation carried on late into the night and by the time that Shirley had emailed Paul giving an update with all of the news and a copy of the note that she had found, it was well into the early hours of the morning before she was able to retire to bed.

The following morning Lillian was woken by a gunshot. Startled, she fumbled her way to the window and drew back the curtains allowing the bright sunlight to come streaming into her room. She could see part of the massive expanse of lawn and just in view was Ian with a gun held in one arm and a dead rabbit swinging from the other. She recalled the comment that Gina had made about him having a competition with the Estate Manager about the number of rabbit pelts that could be collected. Now wide awake she pulled on a dressing gown that had been provided and pulling her bedroom door closed behind her, tapped on Shirley's room and waited for a moment until hearing a muffled voice she went in. The room was in total darkness, the windows effectively covered by long velvet curtains.

The strange combination of words that emerged from the bed included, 'Go away, sleep, late night,' separated by the odd curse or two. Getting the message quickly she retreated back to her room where she got ready for the day ahead. Deciding that she had at least an hour of free time before Shirley emerged she decided to go for a walk in the grounds.

* * *

When she walked out onto the gravel drive there was no-one in sight. Ian had moved on so she decided to follow the route that led down to the lake then up through the rocks to the bridge. It took a little time but eventually, out of breath, she found herself looking down over the waterfall admiring the stunning view that it provided. She sensed, rather than heard, the presence of another person on the bridge and looking up she was dismayed to see the figure of David Motte standing just a few yards away.

His voice was chilling as he spoke to her.

'Our agreement was that you kept me informed of your progress. Sneaking off to Lisbon without telling me makes me think that you are planning on keeping the necklace for yourselves. Or is it that you have come to an agreement with your new friends and you are going to sell it to them? It belongs to my family, the true Order of the Rosicrucians, not these fakes who live here.'

Suddenly she realised that she had been caught up in an internecine war between the two factions. Motte represented the group that she had been told about the previous night and was determined to get hold of the Queen's necklace on their behalf.

Lillian tried to compose herself before she replied, 'I never sneak. We are following up leads and if they had led anywhere, you would have been the first to know.'

Motte's reply scared her even more than the tone of voice in which he spoke.

* * *

'I think that it is time to send a message to Mr. Paul Breslin to make him realise that I am not to be trifled with.'

He reached into his inside pocket and took out a gun that if she hadn't been so afraid, Lillian might have thought was just a toy. Her knowledge of firearms was non existent but she was sure that something so dangerous should have been bigger. As he raised his arm towards her she tried to determine whether she was better off rushing at him or jumping over the bridge into the rushing waters. Before she could decide there was the sound of a gunshot and Motte slumped to the ground with a surprised look on his face.

Looking around, Lillian was astonished at the sight of Gina Beckford striding towards her with a rifle under her arm. *I mustn't do the pathetic woman thing,* she determined to herself before realising that she was shaking all over and needed the side of the bridge for support. Thinking that she was beyond anymore shocks she was stunned to hear Gina's voice a few moments later saying, 'Piece of shit deserved it pointing a gun at you like that. On our estate too. He's had that coming for a long time.'

Looking up she could see Ian emerging from the woods above the bridge and taking in the situation immediately he simply said, 'Get her up to the house. I'll clean up here.'

As they walked back up, Gina explained that only that morning she had decided to join in the hunt for the rabbits that were ruining the garden.

'Didn't expect to find myself shooting a rat as well. If I hadn't seen what was happening, another minute would have been too late. Doing his own dirty work like that wasn't characteristic of the man but it shows how unstable he had become. If we get rid of his gun it will probably be recorded as a tragic shooting accident to an unknown trespasser. He shouldn't have been wandering around while we were shooting rabbits. Alternatively, Ian might just bury him in the woods. We can leave him to sort it out.'

It wasn't long before Gina was pouring Cognac into beautifully cut crystal glasses.

'You and I need it for the shock. She just likes drinking,' she laughed as Shirley walked in to join them. By the time that Ian appeared an hour later the three women were still giggling as Lillian repeated for the third time, 'It was the look of surprise on his face. If he had realised that he'd been shot by a woman he would have been livid.'

Quickly sobering up, they turned to Ian as Gina asked him what he had decided.

'Bury the bugger in the woods. Don't know about you but I haven't seen a stranger wandering around here, even if anybody asks, but if I knew Motte he would have been acting independently.'

The conversation carried on for a while until noticing how quiet Lillian had become, Shirley asked if she was all right.

'I'm fine, but the thought has just occurred to me, that if he had half a brain on him, the file is still in existence, probably being backed up each day. I have still got to sort that out, otherwise, if it gets into the wrong hands I'm in big trouble. Fortunately I have an idea what to do about it but I need to get back to Paris I'm afraid. There is the possibility that he has arranged for it to be sent, automatically, to the authorities after a certain period of time. That's what I would do anyway. Are you OK continuing your search without me. I'm sure that Ian and Gina would act as translators if you need it.'

'Of course we will. You Shirley, are welcome to stay for as long as you wish and if you would like it Lillian, I could drive you to Lisbon airport in about an hour. We just need to check when the next flight to France is. I'm guessing from what you said that you would prefer to go to Paris rather than Nantes this time.'

20

I read the email that I had received from Shirley for the second time, before glancing out of the window at the clouds that were scudding across a leaden, broken sky. She had sent it in the early hours of this morning so she obviously felt that it was important. At last my desk had arrived and been dragged up multiple flights of stairs into my new study. It was an old, battered Victorian piece of furniture, but suddenly this room felt comfortable and in particular it felt as though it belonged to me. I couldn't say the same for the rest of the house but that would come with time. The weather today here in Locquirec was in direct contrast to the blue sky and sunshine that she was obviously enjoying in Sintra. It didn't matter though as I had lots to do and it was unlikely that I would get out for my daily promenade until much later. Gaston had gone back to my chateau in Montignac in the Loire where, I suspect, he was agonising over the decision about where to make his home. I would be surprised if he decided to come to live and work here in the Breton countryside, but then I could see that he would be more at home in Versailles or Paris than he would be even in Montignac. The change of status in his work since staying on with me after William's death meant that he could actually base himself anywhere and I suspect that he only remained at the chateau out of a sense of loyalty. It was definitely time that we had a serious talk. If he were to continue to manage my business affairs as efficiently as he had been doing during the previous twelve months I needed him to be happy. In fact, if he decided to move to his apartment in Versailles, I would have an excuse for more frequent trips to Paris and of course it would be rude not to call in on Alicia whilst I was there.

The email had an attached photograph of a note, possibly written by Antoine, but without anything to compare it with, it was worthless. However, I had a lead to follow up and the simplest way to do it was here on my laptop using the online French telephone directory. The note that Antoine had received in October 1794 had been sent by a man by the name of Guillot who was obviously a close friend. Guillot was a reasonably common surname in France but armed with the directory of Bordeaux I was preparing myself for a day of telephone calls trying to pin down anyone with a family history going back to the 1790's. There were two dozen entries but by lunchtime I had narrowed them down. Many could be scratched off the list immediately but several promised to be worth following up. There were also a number that were simply not at home and needed to be tried again later. It was still blustery, but wrapped in coat and scarf I decided that I had earned some fresh air. I turned right out of the gate this time and stopped to watch some surfers in the distance. I had to admire them in a mad sort of way but it definitely wasn't for me. The path was slightly muddy in places, but before long I came into the small port and found a table on the terrace of the bistro. As always the plat du jour had a limited choice, but it was superb value for money. With a view to my expanding waistline I decided to go for the main course only and chose a seafood salad that I had spied someone eating on the next table. I even chose a carafe of water rather than the house wine, but in reality it was because of the afternoon's work ahead rather than the extra calories. It was not long before I was back outside and continuing along the path to my favourite bench which overlooked a group of small, moored boats. I liked the sound of the wind whistling through the rigging and when the sun did emerge for a brief period of time the sea reflected a brilliant blue. It was time to think. I had to admit to myself that we had made some progress despite the difficulties that we faced. An obscure reference to a Portuguese artist had led us first to Lisbon and then to Sintra. I needed to connect the note that Shirley had found with Antoine and the only way to do that was to find a copy of his handwriting. It's a funny thing that in the 21st century with the digitisation of every document imaginable, true, original research can only be done by getting off one's backside and looking for material that were yet undiscovered, buried away in a family library or an obscure archive. I needed to finish off my phone calls then tomorrow it was time to head for Bordeaux. I felt a frisson of excitement at the thought of tracking down this mysterious Guillot and uncovering his connection to Antoine.

By the end of the day I had two lists, one much much longer than the other. The longest contained the dead ends, people who had no historical connection with Bordeaux or those who were simply not interested in helping my search. I would return to those later if necessary but in the meantime I had three people who had agreed to see me and were from families whose lineage could be traced back through numerous generations. It piqued their curiosity and pride that an English historian might be interested in their family and they had all agreed to unearth any family material that might be relevant. It always amazed me that most families with a history of any kind hoarded letters and papers that were never looked at, just kept safe in boxes and files. Mind you, it would scupper my work if that weren't the case, the material that you got from official archives usually just didn't help. Having said that, Shirley and Lillian had struck gold at the Gulbenkian Museum in Lisbon so maybe it was time to revise my opinions.

The following morning I was up early and enjoyed a spectacular sunrise and I could hear a woodpecker tapping away somewhere in the garden. It was superbly peaceful but soon it was necessary to drive to the nearest town of Guingamp where I could catch the TGV to Rennes. Once there I would change trains and in a few hours would arrive in Bordeaux. I had brought some reading material with me, but before settling down I had a look round. Compared to the train service in the UK this was infinitely better. It was less crowded, much cleaner and bizarrely, the people were much more interesting to watch. For example the business types with their laptops wore suits but no tie. It sounds trivial but I have always thought that it made for a much classier look. A man, probably in his forties, sat opposite me was reading a battered paperback by the writer Jean Christophe Rufin. Again, much classier than the usual garish cover or even worse, than staring at a mobile phone screen like a zombie. The Breton countryside was beautiful as it flew past the window with mist lying across the fields and valleys. I settled down and it wasn't long before I was stood on the next platform waiting for my connection. The second leg was a bit longer but when I walked out of the station in Bordeaux the sky was a brilliant blue and I was having to suppress the excitement that was starting to creep in. This was what I really loved, tracking down forgotten artefacts, gathering missing information then putting it all together to either prove or more frequently, disprove an idea that I had been nurturing. My first appointment was with, not surprisingly, a Madam Guillot and a short taxi ride saw me emerging onto a street just off the Place de la Bourse. The architecture was clearly 18th century and the address that I had been given was that of a grand townhouse. Once again I had to remind myself that the odds were massively against me and sure enough, having spent a pleasant hour with an old lady who enjoyed reminiscing about her family, it turned out to be a dead end. This scenario was repeated a second time at another address in the same area. With this reality check kicking in I walked to the nearby square to get a taxi to the last address. The taxi driver looked at the piece of paper that I gave him and frowned.

'Are you sure Monsieur? This is not an area for tourists. It is down by the docks and is somewhat rough.'

I reassured him that I knew what I was doing and arranged for him to come back to pick me up in an hour's time. Having been brought up in the North of England I have to say that his idea of rough and mine were somewhat at odds with each other. Admittedly the houses were less grand than the ones that I had just visited but when the door was opened by a woman of a similar age to myself, dressed in what I imagined to be Parisian chic street style, I started to apologise explaining that I must have the wrong address. I thought that my French was pretty good but her face lit up with laughter as she replied in perfect English that in fact she was Mademoiselle Guillot and it had been her grandmother that I had spoken to. I was led into a large drawing room at the back of the house which overlooked a beautiful garden. The walls were lined with bookcases and a classic red leather sofa and armchairs were placed towards the centre of the room. The highly polished floorboards were largely covered by an expensive looking, patterned carpet. Having made the introductions Madame Guillot explained that she had asked her granddaughter Sophie along in order to help to get some of the boxes down from the loft where they normally lived. After just a few minutes conversation it looked to me as though I had struck pay dirt. The lady herself was very elegant in both her appearance and her manner, but her descriptions of her family tree led me to think that I was getting closer in my search.

I could see that the corridor which ran off to the right was almost blocked with boxes and it was obvious that it would take several days to go through everything there. I was half listening to a story that Madame Guillot was telling and wondering if I was going to take over this small house when Sophie noticed my gaze and spoke.

'I work for one of the less well known wine chateaux and our headquarters have a number of offices that are not being used at the moment. I will need to check with my boss, but I'm certain that there wouldn't be a problem if a famous historian and writer wanted to use one for a few days. It might even help to publicise our wines.'

I started to thank her but pointed out that it would be a logistical nightmare to persuade a taxi driver to load his cab with the piles of boxes. Once again she surprised me when she said, 'Not a problem. I can get hold of a van and in the morning we can load it up and if grandmama is happy with the idea you can work out at the chateau and we'll bring everything back when you have finished. I just need to make a couple of phone calls.'

While she went into the kitchen to make the calls her grandmother explained that Sophie's work involved publicising their range of wines and that the organisation basically OK'd any suggestion that she made. Another surprise was waiting however, when she said, 'The van is probably from the group. She does a lot of travelling, but when she's at home she plays in a jazz trio at the clubs in town. They normally use the van for carrying their instruments around but they are a lovely bunch and I'm sure that they won't mind.'

I have to confess that I liked the way that this was moving. Pretty, chic and a jazz musician to boot. I needed to remind myself that she was probably involved with somebody and that I was there on business. *Concentrate boy,* I thought to myself.

A few minutes later Sophie returned with a smile on her face and confirmed that it was all set. She checked which hotel I was staying at and arranged that she would pick me up at nine the following morning. I had sent the taxi away earlier after paying him generously for a wasted journey, but as I made a move to ring for another Sophie offered me a lift back into the centre. 'I have an apartment not far from where you are staying so it's no effort to drop you off. By the way, don't organise anything for Friday night. Your online biography says that you like jazz so I have a surprise for you.'

* * *

I stepped out of the hotel on the dot of nine the following morning to see another beautiful day with a brilliant blue sky. It would get much hotter later, but at the moment the air was fresh and cool. A large white Renault van was parked across the road and as I looked, my acquaintance from the previous day opened the door and stepped out of the passenger seat. When I crossed the road she offered her cheek for the traditional 'bise' which fortunately for me followed the pattern in Brittany of two kisses. I had been in Provence once and got into a real tangle when the lady went for a third offering and we spectacularly crashed heads. A moment later the driver's door opened and a large muscular looking man emerged to be introduced as Brian the drummer. 'Drumming gives him massive arms so he will be useful shifting boxes. He also needs the van later so I will take my car out to the vineyard.'

Brian thrust his hand forward and when I took it, it was like shaking hands with a bench vice. I clambered into the passenger seat and we followed Sophie through the traffic to her grandmother's house in the docklands. She explained that Madame Guillot was out that morning so we were able to load up the boxes without interruption. The description of Brian was accurate and he was shifting four boxes to my two. Largely because of his efforts it wasn't long before we were back in the van and again following the orange 2CV out into the countryside. When we eventually pulled off the road, a metalled track led us through acre after acre of grape vines which were beautifully organised and pruned. At the end of each row were planted several rose bushes which, I had been told, were to provide an early warning if blight were to strike. When I said this to Brian he laughed and explained that this was an old wives tale and that modern vineyard managers had much more sophisticated techniques. They were there simply for decoration. The buildings of the estate were all in that beautiful terracotta brick that is so typical of the southern areas of France. We pulled up outside what looked like a reception area and while Sophie introduced me to the man behind the desk Brian busied himself with unloading the collection of boxes into a room at the back. I joined him a few minutes later and again, largely because of his efforts, the van was soon empty and he was ready to make his goodbye.

For most people, sifting through document after document, letter after letter, would be an unbelievably tedious task. I found it to be fascinating and I had to discipline myself to concentrate on looking for material that was relevant and not try to read everything. Time passed quickly and with only a short break to eat a sandwich that Sophie kindly dropped by to leave for me, I found myself making progress. I could see that there would be a few days work ahead of me, but already the boxes were organised into two areas of the room. Those that had been checked - much the smaller of the two and those that hadn't. I learned much about the Guillot family during that first day but nothing that helped in my search for Antoine Lestrade. The next day was much the same except that I insisted on taking Sophie for lunch at the bistro in the local village. We talked easily and I learned that she had been born and educated in Bordeaux, earning a degree in oenology at the university. She had worked for several wineries in the area and had worked herself up to her current position of Estate Manager. The 'boss' of whom she had previously spoken turned out to be the owner of the estate and to all intents and purposes, the day to day running was left to her. It was a wrench to leave but she had work to return to and my search was a long way from being finished.

* * *

It was just before I was due to finish for the day that I had my first success. A bundle of letters fastened together which were addressed simply to 'Guillot'. Opening the first of these I found a short note dated 1806 and sent from Versailles. It was signed 'Ever your friend, Antoine.' The contents described a family event to which Guillot was invited and were largely irrelevant. What was relevant however, was that I now had a copy of Antoine's handwriting and although it would need to be authenticated by an expert, to my untrained eye it matched the handwriting on the letter sent by Shirley a few days earlier. We were making progress. I hadn't heard from Shirley since they had left Lisbon for Sintra so I assumed that they were similarly engaged, ploughing through box after box of papers. Her trip had been slightly speculative so I quickly fired off a copy of the document that I had found giving my opinion of the handwriting match. Before leaving, I looked through the rest of the bundle. After the initial excitement they were a little less interesting and although comprising of several years of correspondence between Antoine and Guillot and making several references to Lisbon and Sintra there was no reference to any jewellery or necklace. I wasn't in the least bit surprised at this but it did motivate me for the rest of the boxes that needed to be tackled tomorrow.

21

Sophie and I chattered non stop on the way back into town. It was Friday evening and the traffic was particularly heavy although I was sorry when we finally approached my hotel. Before dropping me off she gave me clear directions to a club where I was to meet her later that night then leaning across the gap between us kissed my cheek before I got out. I was finding it difficult to believe that we had only met yesterday such was the 'simpatico' between us. I was looking forward to the evening ahead. I had seen a clothes shop just a few blocks away from the hotel and as I had packed lightly for the trip I walked back and bought myself a pair of light coloured chinos and a dark blue shirt. A few other items that I needed went into the bag then it was back to the hotel for a shower. It was still warm when I emerged two hours later. I was due at the Club Avril 21 at nine o'clock, but first I wanted to sample the evening air and sit with a glass of pastis and watch the world go by. I had much to think about but I was fascinated by the groups of people both young and old that promenaded past my table. Friday night in Bordeaux was obviously the place to be. Eventually, I finished my glass and left a few coins on the table. Another ten minutes saw me looking at a garish neon sign reading 21, flashing blue then green and back to blue again. I pushed open the door below the sign and made my way towards the bar that I could see at the back of the place. To the right was a low stage with a piano, a set of drums and a double bass carefully placed on its stand. There were tables around the area in front of the stage, some with reserved notes on them, but of Sophie there was no sign. However, leaning against the bar I could see the bulky figure of Brian the drummer that I had met previously. His greeting was effusive and he insisted on buying me another pastis. The music that was playing through the speakers was fairly loud so he had to raise his voice to make himself heard.

'Of course, I'm playing, Sophie is on bass and you will meet our pianist in a little while.'

I don't know why I was so surprised that Sophie was going to manhandle that beautiful wooden instrument. I guess that I had just not come across female bass players before. I also found out why the club had been named Avril 21. It was in honour of Nina Simone who passed away on that date in 2003 in the South of France. I guess you learn something new every day. It was another surprise when Sophie came in through a side door looking just as gorgeous as she had earlier in the day but more appropriately dressed for an evening of music. I had obviously been promoted from the kiss on the cheek to a full, body melting arms round my waist, hug that seemed to last for a few seconds longer than I anticipated. Not that I am complaining you understand.

Before I had chance to catch my breath she said, 'Enjoy the performance,' and walked between the tables with Brian alongside her.

I hadn't noticed the pianist arrive but he was already sat waiting for the two of them and after a few moments he introduced the group as the David Koz Trio. I was soon lost in the music which sounded like some of the Scandinavian jazz that I loved so much. The pianist, presumably David Koz himself was melodic, Brian's drumming was much more subtle than his size suggested was possible and the bass lines that Sophie developed were ingeniously elegant. The set lasted for an hour in total and they finished with an encore that received rapturous applause. With massive smiles on their faces they walked across to the table where I was seated and joined me. I was pleased that Sophie grabbed the chair next to mine and by the time that they were organised the barman had brought a bottle of red wine and four glasses. Looking at the label I immediately noticed that it was from the vineyard where I had spent the last two days. The two men were immediately kept busy fending off congratulations from the people around us so I took it upon myself to fill the glasses. Wow. I love wine but I had rarely come across this combination of velvet fruit with a tannin bite. Sophie was watching my expression as I took a sip and she asked, 'So what did you think?'.

'You were brilliant. I loved the whole set.'

'Not me you idiot. The wine. It's last year's vintage and I'm trying to persuade some of the supermarket chains to stock it on their shelves. It's a cut throat business and it's difficult to survive without the exposure that you get from these shops.'

* * *

I smiled then repeated, 'You were brilliant. The wine's not bad either.' I received a punch on the arm for my troubles as David and Brian turned back round and they started to analyse the evening's music.

'Boring, boring, boring,' was Sophie's response and with a glance at me said, 'Paul's taking me for a meal to pay off his debt so we are going to leave you two to the mercy of this lot.'

It was news to me, but I was never one to pass up an opportunity. We made our goodbyes and as we stepped out of the door Sophie took my arm and steered me down the street.

'You have two choices. We can either stop at a restaurant or order a Thai food delivery at my apartment?'

This was moving fast but as I was only likely to be here for another day or so, I decided to do the honourable thing.

'I guess it's your apartment then.'

I am far too much of a gentleman to do 'kiss and tell' reveals, but suffice it to say that I thoroughly enjoyed my Thai meal and in the morning we were slow to emerge. I needed to get back to the hotel before heading on out to the winery and although it was Sophie's weekend, she elected to drive me to the hotel to pick up my notes and MacBook before setting off for the estate.

By now it was much later than our usual start and the sun was higher in the sky and insisted on playing hide and seek with the white clouds that were scudding above the buildings. Today was slightly different in that instead of going in to work she dropped me off then went back into town with an arrangement to collect me later. My habitual excitement when on the track of history must be likened sadly to that felt by the local hunters when they are on the scent of wild boar. As I sat down I could feel my pulse quicken. Today would be the day when Antoine's secrets would be exposed to me. I was confident.

Three hours later I was no closer in my hunt for this bloody necklace. The story of Antoine's escape and his friendship with Guillot that came to light was fascinating and given the right circumstances I was sure that I could turn out a story that my publishers would love. The problem was that there wasn't a single mention of this piece of jewellery. It must be, as I had suspected all along, that the letter that Motte had based everything on was misinformed. Either that or, more likely, Antoine was too cautious to reveal anything in his correspondence. I say more likely because he had not been candid about his escape from Versailles and eventual exodus to Portugal. There was even a mention of Guillot's occupation of 'Gentleman Thief' before he had settled down as a legitimate businessman here in Bordeaux. This of course had massive implications for Lillian. Gaston's sister had brought this situation down on herself by virtue of her own stupidity, but we had all been there as rebellious kids. She didn't deserve to serve a lengthy prison sentence, but I really couldn't see a way out of this. Even if we adopted Patrice's solution of a nudge in the back by a busy road, Lillian had made it clear that Motte would have been clever enough to automate the release of the file at some point in the future. I was also puzzled by his motivation. Was he so deranged as to believe that this necklace really belonged to him and his family and what if he did get his hands on it. Even after three hundred years it would be instantly recognisable and certainly unsaleable. I suppose that it could be broken down and the diamonds sold separately but what a travesty of history that would be. I had a superb story laid out in front of me, but no idea where to look next. There were still two more boxes to examine before I was finished, but I held out little hope. The only positive thing to have come out of all of this was that I had met Sophie and that I now had a good excuse to come back and spend more time here. Oh yes - and I could sense another best seller on the horizon.

As I suspected the remaining material filled in some gaps in Antoine's later life and actually included a direct reference to the portrait that had originally pointed us at Lisbon, but that was all. Every box had been thoroughly examined, the documents and letters placed back exactly as they were and they now stood complete against one wall. This trail was over. It was possible that Shirley might have more news, but she had been suspiciously quiet over the last few days so I was not optimistic about her progress. I had an hour to kill before I was due to be collected so I ventured outside to walk and appreciate the estate. The fields rolled away into the distance and I admired the well kept, organised rows of vines that would produce the next vintage. The soil was dry and flinty but I had read somewhere that this was the 'terroir' that enabled the grapes to achieve their maximum flavour. If the bottle that I had tasted last night was anything to go by it certainly worked well. The clouds had disappeared by now and the heat was intense so I went back inside and composed emails to Gaston and Shirley summarising my findings. I guess it was back to the drawing board.

We were due to return the boxes to her mother the next day so with the rest of today to kill, Sophie took it upon herself to show me the delights of Bordeaux. It's a great city to walk around with a fantastic coffee society and some beautiful buildings. We sat and drank at pavement café's and generally enjoyed each others company. I had almost forgotten the real reason that I was here when my phone pinged and I checked the text message that had arrived. Shirley had finally made contact, but I was surprised by the message. 'Lillian has left for Paris. Don't want to risk email but I have some people that you should meet. Any chance you can fly to Lisbon?'

Bugger. Back to reality for me. Sophie saw the expression on my face and guessed that all was not well. I decided that it was time to come clean. An hour later I could see that she was not happy about being deceived as I explained that Lillian's freedom was at stake and as she had been a stranger just a few days ago, it had been expedient for me to go with the cover story. After what had happened since, I explained, I was certain that I could now trust her. I knew that she hadn't really forgiven me when she didn't invite me back to her apartment but walked me back to the hotel. She had argued that I should get the flight the next day and that she didn't need me to help to return the boxes to her grandmother's. 'After all, it was Brian that did most of the work last time.'

It was a slightly strained goodbye as she reverted to the kiss on the cheek and wished me good luck. I promised to be in touch and turned to enter the hotel. Bugger again. I seemed to be incapable of maintaining any kind of relationship with a woman.

I was puzzled and there were a stack of unanswered questions. Why had Lillian left for Paris? Why could Shirley not explain herself by phone or email and who on earth were these people that she wanted me to meet? I would be in Lisbon by lunchtime tomorrow and if necessary I could get out to Sintra by the evening so I would have my answers soon enough. In the meantime I had an evening alone to kill. The meal in the hotel restaurant was pleasant enough and I sat in the lounge with my notes, jotting down a combination of ideas for my next book and random thoughts on our current situation. After a while I realised that I was stumped as far as the latter went and that I was much better off organising my plans for a biography of a lawyer who escaped the French Revolution. It could be a great fresh angle to explore a period of history that had really been done to death.

From the material that I had examined it appeared that Antoine was a friend of Robespierre and had prosecuted the famous mathematician Joseph Fourier. There was a tenuous connection with the infamous Queen's necklace but even without that, there was an enormous amount of material to get my teeth into. I felt sorry for Lillian but apart from the fact that she was Gaston's estranged sister there was little reason for me to have become involved. My curiosity had been piqued by the rest of the story though. And what was it that Shirley had discovered that was so important. I trusted her instincts and it was enough that she had asked me to fly into Lisbon at such short notice; even if it meant that Sophie had done an about turn, or was it more likely that I had not told her the true reason for my visit in the first place?

France is full of small regional airports that mean that getting around Europe is fairly easy. They are not big on facilities, but unless you want to buy designer clothing at vastly inflated prices, they are fine. The next morning saw me leaving Bordeaux on the short flight to Lisbon. I was planning to catch a taxi out to Sintra and then work out how to get up to the estate where Shirley was staying when I got there. Instead I was pleasantly surprised to see Shirley and a tall elegant looking woman waiting for me as I emerged from arrivals. I hadn't seen Shirley for some months but she was as smiley and effusive as ever. She introduced her companion as Gina Beckford whose husband Ian, was related to the infamous William Beckford.

They had driven down to collect me and so an hour later I found myself exiting the car in front of a most magnificent house which sat in acres of wonderful estate. During the ride Shirley had talked about her recent doings with Andres in Granada and about some of the paintings that she was working on, but when I asked her about the events here in Portugal she wouldn't answer, simply explaining that the story was Ian's to tell and that I would have to wait until I met him. He was visiting a friend at the moment but would be back that evening for dinner. It didn't take long to unpack the few things that I had with me and when I had finished Gina suggested that Shirley should show me around. The interior of the house was spectacular. I call it a house but in reality it was almost palace like in both its size and its setting. We strolled into the gardens and I made to walk across the lawn down to the lake and towards a waterfall that I could see in the distance. A strange expression passed across her face and as she took my arm she made to move in a different direction. My curiosity went off the Richter scale when she told me that she would explain the significance of the bridge that evening, but that she would prefer to avoid it at the moment. The rest of the day passed pleasantly, but I was desperate for the evening to start in order to find out what strange events had brought me here.

At eight o'clock, I left my room and walked down a

magnificent staircase in the direction of the drawing room. I remembered that it was on the right hand side of the long corridor but I wasn't sure which door to try. My first effort led into a magnificent library and I paused to admire the shelves of leather bound volumes that stretched from floor to ceiling.

'Good Evening. You must be Paul. I have heard a lot about you and I'm delighted that you were able to come at such short notice. I'm Ian Beckford and this is my home.'

There was a leather chair which was in silhouette from the bright evening sun and it's occupant was all but invisible to me. I started to apologise for intruding but he graciously brushed my apologies aside.

'I stopped in here to look something up but let's join the others and get ourselves a drink.'

He stood up, put a book back into a gap on one of the shelves and strode across with his hand outstretched. I could now see a man in his fifties, smart looking in old cord trousers and a white shirt. His red framed glasses were very distinctive and gave an artistic edge to an aristocratic bearing.

'I'm sorry that I wasn't able to meet you earlier but I've been out arranging something that you might find interesting. Anyway, we have lots to talk about so those details will keep until then.'

His accent was more Oxbridge than Portuguese and I later learned that he did indeed study at Cambridge. The familiarity with which he put one hand on my shoulder whilst shaking with the other however, was definitely more

Portuguese than Oxbridge.

He guided me out of the library and into the drawing room where Shirley and Gina Beckford were sat talking. Drinks and then dinner passed with no attempt to alleviate my curiosity. I answered questions about my books, we talked about our mutual love of art, but eventually we returned to the drawing room and with drinks in hand Ian at last said, 'Now. It is time to tell you a story.'

22

He talked about the history of his family starting with the eccentric aristocrat William Beckford and gave a timeline through to the present day. It was William that interested me the most of course, but it was difficult to decide whether this was because I was entangled in Lillian's current situation or simply the fact that I could smell another historical biography. Exiled from England because of numerous scandals, polymath, host to many of the great and the good of his time and owner of one of the largest estates in the area there was a wealth of material here. However, what really caught my attention was when Ian began to talk about a mysterious organisation that he called the Rosicrucians. His description gave them a historical context with connections to the Royal Society whilst making them sound like a more altruistic version of the freemasons. It was no surprise to hear that William Beckford had been a member nor that Ian and Gina were members also. The bombshell came though when he explained that the late William Scott, a man that I had regarded almost as my grandfather, had also been a Rosicrucian. I guessed that it was supposed to give them more credibility in my eyes, but in reality I had always been suspicious of so called secret societies believing them to be secretive for a reason. His description of two factions was credible enough, but I was suspicious of the angle that 'we are good and they are bad'. My experience of these things was that it was impossible to be just black or white and that there were always a multitude of shades in between.

I now understood why Shirley had asked me to come in person. This was obviously a recruiting drive on their part and although she trusted them, I was of a much more cynical nature. It was turning into a night of surprises and the fact that I accepted an offer to be a guest at one of their meetings was, perhaps to me, the biggest surprise of all. I must admit that the fact that it was being held in the famous Initiation Well at the nearby Quinta da Regaleira that added to my curiosity. I had read about the estate when I was researching Antoine Lestrade's possible connection to the area. It was a mysterious place with lakes, grottoes and fountains but the so called Initiation Well had grabbed my interest. It was, in effect, an inverted tower spiralling into the ground with a winding staircase which led down through nine platforms. The number was supposedly symbolic of Dante's Divine Comedy with the nine circles of hell and nine skies of paradise. Both masonic and templar symbols added to the air of mystery that supposedly surrounded the place. I really couldn't be done with the mumbo jumbo that Ian was using to try to persuade me, but as a historian I was fascinated by the structure and welcomed the chance to see it for myself.

There was one last shock to complete the night and that was

Shirley's description of the visit of David Motte. The fact that he had pointed a gun at Lillian was more than justification, in my eyes, for Gina's action. I made it clear that I was not interested in how they had dealt with the body. His death was no loss to me although when Shirley described the potential issue of a time delay that might later automatically release the file to the authorities, I was more concerned. It wasn't something that I had experience of, but she had spoken to Andres who had confirmed that not only was it possible, it was the most obvious thing to have done. Not surprisingly, after Shirley's incarceration the previous year he had been livid that she had been close to a similar situation again. It had taken some persuasion on her part to convince him that Motte's death had removed any possible danger to herself and that she was simply going to finish off the research before returning to Granada.

It had been a long day and an evening that had been full of revelations so I was the first to make my apologies and retire back upstairs. I intended to spend tomorrow helping Shirley to finish the research here and then the following day I had an invitation to a special meeting.

I was awake early the next morning so before breakfast I strolled down to the lake, but this time turned towards the bridge from which I had previously been diverted. I could see why Shirley might want to avoid it, but I was of a different ilk. Climbing up the path through the rocks I saw the area where Gina must have stood looking upwards towards the two figures. It wasn't an angle that afforded a great view so it struck me that she must be a pretty good shot to have hit Motte from here. At the top the bridge ran across a stream that itself tumbled down into the lake. There was literally nothing to see and if any investigation did lead to the

Estate a simple plea of ignorance by Ian, one of the local aristocrats, would be more than sufficient. I would doubt that Motte would have given out details of his movements if he had been planning to menace or injure Lillian. It was just the complication of this bloody file now. I could offer no help, but I was keen to stay on the tenuous trail of Antoine Lestrade and his increasingly unlikely connection to the necklace. I was enjoying the early morning sun, but eventually I strode back and walked past the terrace and through the double doors. The breakfast room was empty although there were still fresh rolls and a variety of cereals and coffee on a side table so I helped myself and sat down.

Whilst I ate I thumbed through my notebook and was acutely aware of how little progress had been made towards finding the necklace. With some difficulty we had followed the path of Antoine from Versailles here to Sintra, but had found no reference at all to the artefact. Unless today brought something new to light I decided that I would declare it over and concentrate on making a start on the biography of Antoine Lestrade. I hoped that something could be done to help Lillian, but that was way beyond my area of expertise.

After finishing a second cup of coffee I made my way to the library and pushing the door open I found Shirley hard at work already. She cheerily called out a good morning and started to explain how she had been going about the task and which shelves still needed to be investigated. There appeared to be little order to the books and boxes of files so it was a slow and painstaking job to read through material that had been written in a language that I didn't understand, simply looking for names that I recognised. Most of the books could be dealt with quickly by checking that no sheets of paper were left between pages or that no annotation had taken place. I found several with handwritten notes, but they were all outside our timeframe so I didn't bother to find Ian or Gina to translate.

The morning passed slowly until when we were left with just one line of box files, I declared a lunch break. Ian had popped in a couple of times to see how we were getting on and to remind me that the following evening he and I were due at the Quinta da Regaleira. He profusely apologised to Shirley, but explained that it was a men only event, a fact that made me even more uneasy. I had occasionally come across 'men only' bars at golf clubs or received invitations to 'men only' book events. It definitely wasn't something that I either liked or approved of but my curiosity about the Initiation Well overcame my reluctance.

I was also fascinated by the fact that the well had been originally used for an initiation ceremony by the infamous Hellfire Club. According to Ian, they had been hounded out of London because of their activities and so various members had set up replicas across Europe, Sintra being one of them. It had been some years afterwards that the local Rosicrucian Society had taken it over when the estate had been purchased by Regaleira.

The afternoon yielded further disappointment when we found nothing of interest in the remaining files. As far as this lead was concerned we had reached a dead end. I was committed to staying for one more day and Shirley had decided that she wanted to return home as soon as possible. She had been extremely thorough and I made a mental note to add a generous bonus to her fee. I could see that she was irritated about being excluded from the meeting the following evening, but I suspected that my invitation had only arisen because of my connection with William plus any influence that I might be able to wield because of my background. I had no intention whatsoever of joining, my feelings being the same as those of Groucho Marx. 'I wouldn't want to join any club that would have me as a member'.

It had been fun to meet up again but the following morning she hugged me goodbye and made me promise to come to Granada soon. I watched her get into the car and a few seconds later Gina was driving her back to Lisbon airport. Despite being unable to find a connection to the missing necklace, I had amassed a volume of material on Antoine and in my mind I was starting to put together the story of a man who had been forced to flee the Reign of Terror in 1794. There were still unanswered questions and big gaps to fill but I had enough material to make a start. Lillian was still a problem to be solved, but by now I was of a mind to pass the problem on to Guilbert and Patrice. It was perhaps something that they would be able to deal with now that my search had failed. The death of David Motte complicated things enormously and I'm afraid that I was of the opinion that the world had been significantly improved by his demise. I hadn't heard from Lillian since her departure to Paris and I wasn't receiving any replies to my messages. She had told Shirley that she was going to sort it out herself so I would give it until I returned to Brittany before asking for their help.

The following day was particularly quiet but it gave me an opportunity to start writing an outline of the ideas that I had. My publisher would be happy with most things that I proposed but a popularist story such as this would delight him. Towards the end of the afternoon Ian joined me to go through the plans for the evening. We would leave for the Initiation Well at nine o'clock and all that he asked of me was to keep an open mind. There were several people that wished to talk to me and if I would just hear them out, I could then stay or leave as I wished.

At the set time I emerged dressed as always in chinos and shirt and although the sun was low in the sky, the heat of the day was being radiated back from the landscape. Ian insisted that I borrow a waxed jacket which he assured me that I would be glad of. It was just a ten minute drive to the Quinta and as we passed through the gates I could see that the estate was several orders of magnitude grander than his. The house was much more like a palace and the grounds looked as though they were tended by an army of gardeners. We parked the car amongst several dozen others amongst which, I could see a number that would probably cost more than the house in which most people lived. I was obviously going to spend an evening in the company of some obscenely wealthy people. Why on earth they would want to travel to the edge of Europe and participate in some obscure rights of passage, I couldn't possibly imagine.

Ian obviously caught my train of thought and commented, 'Inherited money gives a different perspective on things and I include myself amongst that group. We are able to live our life in a way that wouldn't be considered normal by most people.'

The frightening thought occurred to me that I had also obtained my wealth by inheritance although it had happened recently enough to give me some sort of balance and perspective. I remembered what he had said earlier, listen to what they had to say and leave. I was determined to see what I could of the main Initiation Well as I suspected that it had played a part in Antoine's story. It was funny how I had recently become on first name terms with a man who had been dead for three hundred years.

The path that we followed led away from the Palace and through a wooded area which opened out onto a gravelled terrace. An inauspicious low wall marked the edge of the well. I could hear music emanating from the hole in the ground, a chant of sorts that sounded medieval in origin. Ian led the way to an opening in the wall and I could look down into the well. I had never seen anything like it before. It is referred to as a well, but with the staircase spiralling down through alcoves and balconies it much more resembled a tower that had been inverted into the ground. Down at the very bottom, a cross that I recognised as being affiliated with the Knights Templar was laid out in a pattern on the tiled floor. The chanting was much louder now and if the intention of these people was to create an atmosphere of uneasiness and edginess, they had certainly succeeded as far as I was concerned and I was only a guest. Ian led the way and I realised that three large gentlemen in black suits were following behind.

Ian turned and spoke, 'Trust me. This is a special occasion and I would not allow any harm to befall you. I want you to see what is below and then you can make up your own mind whether to stay or to return.'

I think that this unnerved me more than it offered any kind of reassurance, but my curiosity encouraged me to follow in his footsteps. I was soon glad of the jacket that he had loaned me as the walls were dripping with humidity and more than once large drops of water splashed onto me from above. At the bottom the music could be heard from all three tunnels that led away into semi darkness and following Ian I turned left and walked for a short distance, finding myself in a large chamber that had been carved out of the rock. The light that was given off from the electric bulbs that had been strung along the rock wall was stark, dark shadows contrasting with regions that were glaringly bright. Standing waiting for us was the owner of the estate, the Baron da Regaleira. He introduced himself to me and in English, tinged with a strong Portuguese accent, started to tell me about this blasted Society of Rosicrucians. I had heard much of the story from Ian the previous evening but I really began to pay attention when he started talking about the Queen's necklace.

To cut a long story short, his claim was that the stones from the necklace were originally provided by his organisation and thus it rightfully belonged to them when found. In return for my part in restoring it to its rightful owners I would be welcomed into the Order with all of the benefits that men of power such as himself could bestow upon me. He hinted that some of the benefits available were not for 'ordinary people' and that the laws of the land did not really apply to them anyway. I was not in a position to provoke him with outright skepticism with our escort stood close behind him, but I did explain in some detail of the search that we had carried out and the conclusion that I had reached that the necklace had been lost forever. I was obviously very persuasive because eventually he stopped me with a gesture and turned and spoke.

'I told you David that this was not going to work. I suggest that you pass the girl onto the authorities then wash your hands of the whole business.'

* * *

You can imagine my astonishment when a middle aged man with a plump face stepped out from the shadows. It didn't need Beckford to introduce him to me as I had Googled him as soon as I had started receiving his text messages. Stood in front of me was a man who had started all of this, a man who I believed to be dead, a man who was known as David Motte.

His explanation was childishly simple if somewhat incredible to believe. It had originally been Beckford's idea to get us on to their side. Pretend to save Lillian from Motte and our gratitude would mean that I would make an extra effort to find the necklace and hand it over to them. I had obviously done too good a job in persuading them that I had no interest in pursuing this quest any further and that I certainly had no interest in this club of theirs. So here I was, at the bottom of the Initiation Well with Motte, Beckford, Regaleira and three heavies.

It was Motte that asked the question. 'The thing is Mr. Breslin, what should we do with you.'

23

You can imagine that I was not in a comfortable position, either literally or figuratively. The atmosphere was dank and dark and in my view my prospects were not great. Even so I was astonished at the casual way that Regaleira instructed his minders.

'Get rid of him and dispose of the body.'

I turned to run but the figure in front had already pulled out a firearm which he was pointing in my direction. I discovered at this juncture that the natural human inclination was to try to maintain the status quo for as long as possible. Better to die later than immediately. I started to argue that everyone knew where I was, but I was pushed from behind in the direction of the exit. I couldn't decide whether my anger was because I had been naive enough to put myself in this position or because of the casual way they intended to end my life. Whichever it was, there was little that I could do about it.

If I were being dramatic I would claim that the trek back to the staircase had taken forever. We arrived there in just a few minutes and for the life of me, quite literally in fact, I couldn't see a way out of my dilemma. I had also thought of a third reason for my anger. I had a book to write. I really wanted to tell Antoine's story, but at this moment it was looking seriously unlikely. I walked as slowly as they would allow, resting on each level. I tried to talk some kind of reason into them, but either they spoke no English or they were totally ignoring me. Three levels from the top and I was really getting worried. It's amazing how the brain doesn't believe the inevitable until it becomes so close as to be almost tangible. Two levels to go and I was becoming frantic. I had tried shouting for help, but I simply received a slap across my ears that made my head ring. I paused for the last time before we would exit above ground. The air had become warmer, the humidity had disappeared and the stars were shining brightly in the night sky. The estate was large and I guessed that I would be killed and buried somewhere here. It was probably less of a risk for them than taking an unwilling prisoner off site. The shove in my back told me that it was time to move. It was as we reached the last few steps that it all happened. I had one of the thugs in front of me leading the way and two following behind. Why they thought that I needed an escort of three people I couldn't imagine. One on his own would have been more than enough.

The man in front clambered up the last few steps and had just started to emerge onto level ground when a figure stood up from behind the retaining wall, put his foot into his chest and pushed. Hard. So hard in fact that with a stifled cry he fell sideways over the edge and dropped many metres to the bottom of the well. I didn't see what had happened to him because a second figure stood up above me and pointed a gun at the nearest of the thugs behind me. Unfortunately for him he was the one carrying a gun of his own which he had to swing upwards in order to defend himself. Too late, as I heard a muffled noise and he slumped to the floor. I was still absorbing what had happened when the third thug behind me shouted in French telling me to get up and out. I didn't need to be told twice and I ran upwards.

'No time for explanations. Come quickly.'

Patrice - yes Patrice, exchanged a quick hug with the man behind me then turned and led the way back towards the Palace. I was ushered into a hire car and we flew down the long drive and out onto the road. For the first few kilometres, Patrice who was next to me in the rear seat sat with his neck twisted watching the road behind. Guilbert was driving like a maniac or as he told me later, like a professional. It was only when we had reached the autoroute that they relaxed and started to answer my questions. They had arrived just in time because first of all, Shirley, who I had thought had trusted the Beckford's, had in fact been extremely suspicious of their attempts to get me to the initiation ceremony by myself. Before flying out to Granada she had phoned Gaston who in turn had spoken to Guilbert and Patrice. At about the same time they had also received a call from the man who now sat in the front passenger seat. He had once been in the special services with my two friends and when the unit had been disbanded had started work as a mercenary. His current contract had been with the Baron da Regaleira and when he had overheard a conversation in which my name had been the prime topic of interest he had contacted his old comrades. I couldn't believe the coincidence but I was reassured that they had contacts all over Europe and all kept closely in touch. Another mental note was made to upgrade their salaries. I didn't need their primary skills very often, but when I did I really needed them. I thanked them profusely, but the only gruff response that I got was that Philippe was now out of work so if I heard about anyone needing his talents could I let them know. It seemed that this again was an example of Guilbert's peculiar sense of humour as they all immediately burst into roars of laughter. I was told that in fact all of them were in great demand and could walk into any one of a dozen contracts the next day. I asked why then they stayed in my employ and Patrice, trying to regain his composure replied, 'Fewer bullets flying around, Patron.'

This set them off again and I was able to get little sense out of them until we approached the airport. They quickly became serious and gave me very precise instructions about leaving the car and entering the airport terminal.

'I have to get rid of this gun, but then when we are inside, we should be safe enough. That mob aren't likely to risk provoking the armed police in there.'

Philippe escorted me from the dropping off point while Patrice and Guilbert went to dispose of the gun and to return the hire car. A half hour later the four of us were sat comfortably in the departure lounge. My friends had sensibly picked up my passport and luggage as they had driven past Beckford's house balancing the ten minute delay that it caused them with the practicality of getting out of the country quickly. The house had been empty which was probably fortunate for anyone that might have confronted them. The only flight that suited that day was to Paris, so it was a bit of a dog leg and after saying goodbye to Philippe at Charles de Gaulle airport, then catching the TGV to Rennes and on to Guingamp where we were collected by Gaston.

All in all it had been an interesting day. One of my first jobs was to telephone Shirley to thank her for her quick thinking. It had almost certainly saved my life.

So it seemed that we were back where we had started. Lillian was out of touch, Motte was back on the scene and would almost certainly start his threats again, but this time probably releasing the file on Lillian. Added to that was the fact that he was not working alone, but as part of a powerful organisation. There was no chance of finding this necklace, so all in all we were actually in a worse position than when it had all started. Not surprisingly Gaston was worried about his sister. The first that he knew of her leaving Lisbon was when Shirley had spoken to him regarding her concerns about my so called 'initiation'.

The best that we could do was to spend the night here then set off for Versailles in the morning. There was always the possibility that she was using it as her base, but if so it made no sense to remain out of communication. Despite our worries it was a no brainer that we spent the evening in the bistro down in the port. Although I had only having been away for a few days it felt wonderful to be walking along the cliff top path with my friends. It was a beautiful evening so we took a table outside and ordered copious carafes of the house red, this was despite Gaston's protestations that I was being cheapskate by not buying the most expensive

Burgundy on the menu. Both Patrice and Guilbert silenced him quickly by declaring their preference for the 'vin de pays', the drink of the peasants. 'We are 'paysans' my friend, men of the earth and proud of it,' and then immediately contradicted themselves by consuming vast quantities of oysters. They loved Gaston but obviously had no time for his pretensions.

Eventually we made our way back to the house and settled down for the night. It had been a long day and sleep was much needed.

The following morning came too quickly. Once again I was setting out without knowing how long I would be away and not really having any idea of what to pack. Consequently I adopted my usual technique of concentrating on my laptop and cables then at the last minute throwing a few other items of clothing into a holdall. It would be enough for a few days and if we were away for any longer then I would be buying again. Patrice and Guilbert had decided that they were staying with us for the time being and I was certainly not going to argue with them.

The drive up to Versailles was a complete contrast to yesterday's blast to Lisbon airport. Gaston had insisted that he come along, which as it was his apartment seemed reasonable enough. However, it was an extra person for them to look out for, not that they acknowledged this. Their competence when things turned sour was frightening in its intensity. They seemed able to switch from jovial villagers to men of violence in moments. We made a couple of stops en route, mainly so that I could get out and stretch. Two days of travelling was beginning to tell. We parked the car in the usual car park and made our way to the apartment block.

The concierge was as professional as usual and answered our questions courteously but was unable to give us any useful information. It seemed that Lillian had not been here in the last few days which meant that it had been a wasted journey. At this point I acknowledged that a phone call would have elicited the same result, but I had been certain that she would have called in here after leaving Lisbon. Then I remembered the side door. Guilbert had replaced the locks but Lillian must have a key. Although I felt that we were being overly cautious, we used the staircase rather than the lift to reach the top floor and sure enough, when we checked the rooms, there were signs that Lillian had been here recently. We had certainly washed up everything when we had left last time but there were mugs and plates that had been used since then. Gaston was less than impressed and immediately started to return the apartment to its usual pristine condition. Of course we were no nearer finding her than when we had left Locquirec that morning. Patrice quickly persuaded me that she might have returned to her old haunts or even to Motte's house, particularly as she believed him to be dead. He also put forward a powerful case for letting the professionals take over in the search. Of course, not only did he mean the two of them, but also the dozens of contacts that they had in the capital. In fact it needed just a half dozen telephone conversations for him to find not only Motte's home address, but also the building in which his employees were turning out computer viruses and malware that were raking in vast profits from innocent users.

'OK, they are our starting points tomorrow.' A conversation followed which basically comprised of Gaston and I arguing that we wanted to go with them and Patrice and Guilbert arguing more forcefully that there was no chance. They eventually won the day by claiming that some of the 'contacts' that they would need to use would be less than comfortable with the presence of two strangers.

'You should be safe enough if you stay in here until we return. The private door would need explosives to get through it now and the concierge on the main entrance is a 24 hour service. There is plenty of food here, just don't go out until we return.'

I remembered a phrase that William had used several times before he died last year. 'Why have a dog and bark yourself'. I'm not sure that either of the gentlemen in front of me would have appreciated being called a dog, but I could see the sense of what he had said. Gaston prepared an evening meal that was astonishingly good considering that much of it had been in the freezer before he started and we retired early with a busy day ahead for at least two of us. It was as I was unpacking the few things that I had brought with me that my mobile phone buzzed and when I looked there was a message from Sophie Guillot down in Bordeaux.

'Ring me when you can. Found another box hidden away in grandmama's attic. Contents look old.'

I wasted no time and rang immediately. I hoped that she had forgiven me a little since I saw her last, but I couldn't really tell from the tone of her voice. She was quite excited by the find which had been discovered when they were stacking the last of the old material that I had been going through. Brian, the drummer had carried the boxes up to the attic and had become intrigued by a pile of old furniture that had been stored there some time in the past. When he started rummaging, he had found the another box that had been missed.

* * *

'I'm no expert Paul but I had a quick look and the contents appear to be quite old. There are several books and stacks of letters that are bundled together.'

When I suggested that I pay a visit the following day, Saturday, she was happy to agree as she wouldn't be at work. After finishing the call I knocked on the room that Patrice and Guilbert were using and asked if they could drop me off at the Gare Saint-Lazare in the morning in order to catch the early TGV down to Bordeaux.

'Should be safe enough Patron. The railway stations are guarded almost as well as airports these days. Let us know which train you are coming back on and one of us will meet you.'

I was touched by their concern for my welfare and readily agreed. I just needed to let Gaston know that he would be on his own tomorrow and possibly, the day after as well. I was always the optimist as far as women were concerned.

The next morning we were out early and with the light traffic at that time of day I was soon stood drinking coffee and reading that day's edition of Le Monde newspaper at one of the station café's. I remembered a painting by Monet that I had seen a few years ago showing the station largely obscured by smoke which had been discharged from the steam trains. It was certainly a lot cleaner today. The journey was just three hours so it was still only mid morning when I emerged from Bordeaux station to look for Sophie. After an exchange of text messages while I was in transit she insisted that she would meet me and more importantly for me, that she had forgiven me.

* * *

I had left instructions with the others that they were to keep me in touch with what was happening in Paris, but unsurprisingly there was nothing yet. Sophie looked as gorgeous as I remembered her, this time wearing just jeans with a linen jacket over black shirt. Simple but stylish. She grabbed my arm explaining that she had moved the box to her apartment and that I was welcome to look at the material there. Things really were looking up. While we walked she insisted on hearing about everything that had happened to me in Lisbon, so with as much exaggeration as possible, trying to make my part sound much more heroic than it actually was, I told her the tale of our escape from the clutches of the 'dastardly villains'. I'm not sure how much of it she believed, but she seemed to appreciate the story. Her apartment was on the top floor of an old converted mill that had been modernised in that industrial style that was so popular a year or two ago. There were long windows on each brick wall so it was flooded with light, but it also meant that you could leave them open to allow a cooling breeze to blow through. The box had been placed on a table in the kitchen so while she filled the coffee pot I opened it up to see what was inside. I had to admit to myself that I wasn't particularly optimistic, but there was little that I could do to help in Paris and the opportunity to see Sophie again was too good to turn down.

There were a large number of letters that had been tied together with twine, but the majority were dated over a century too late. I did become excited by one packet that contained several that had been signed by Antoine, but sadly they were just friendly updates of his life in Versailles and Paris. Eventually after several hours there were just the books that I hadn't examined. The first three were of no relevance and the last was a family bible. I flicked through it but without expecting anything of interest. It was often the case that these old bibles served as family histories and this was no exception. Despite all the research material that I had examined I had never seen a first name for Antoine's friend. He was always just referred to as 'Guillot' but in the pages that had been left blank at the back of this large tome, there were scribbled notes referring to events that had taken place over the years. There was also a family tree that had been started in 1805 by a certain 'Paul Guillot'. It was then that I had a lightbulb moment.

24

I never claim to be a genius, but one of my talents is to be able to recognise links between different strands of information, usually links that are obscure enough that most people wouldn't see a connection. I think of them as lightbulb moments, the instant that the light bulb is switched on and the truth is illuminated. This time however, a child could have seen it and probably a lot more quickly than I had. Most families with any sort of history have a family bible that is handed on from generation to generation. I hadn't seen one in Gaston's apartment so where was it? I had already been invited to spend the night with Sophie rather than booking into a hotel so I needed to let him know that I wouldn't be back that day. During the conversation I asked him about the missing bible, but his reply was rather discouraging.

'We are a family of atheists and I don't remember ever seeing a bible in here. I'll have another look in the attic space though. There is an accumulation of years of junk up there and when I checked before I was looking for documents not a bible.'

There was little else to be done so I gave my full attention to Sophie. I have already said that I'm not a kiss and tell man so I'm afraid that your imagination needs to come into play for a little while.

The following morning we ate croissant and drank coffee while the sun shone brightly. There was some bad news though. She had just heard that her employer was putting the vineyard up for sale and that he couldn't guarantee that her job would be safe.

'The big producers already have their own staff doing the same thing as me so the chances are that I will be looking for employment in the near future.'

Despite that she was still upbeat although a little sad at my departure. I insisted that we said goodbye here and then made my way to the station alone. Again it was an early start and after a flurry of text messages it was arranged that I would be met in Paris by Patrice. As he drove me back to Versailles he updated me on the progress with Lillian's search. They had arranged for the house and the workplace to be watched around the clock but as yet, nothing unusual had occurred. As far as they could tell Motte was still in Portugal. So where was Lillian? We drove to Versailles much more slowly than when we had left. The mid-morning traffic around the Peripherique was horrendous and reminded me of why I preferred to live in Brittany. When we arrived, Gaston was just emerging from the attic with a look of triumph on his face. He thrust a large leather bound book at me saying, 'Here. You will be the first to open it for years. I told you that we are a family of atheists.'

I carefully carried it to a table in the dining room and sat down. Flicking through it I could see that it had been heavily annotated and sure enough the back few blank pages were covered in handwriting. The annotation simply appeared to be someone's irritation with certain verses but the back was fascinating. In a hand that had now become familiar was a page with a heading that translated to, *'Draft Will of Antoine Lestrade'* and dated April 1830. I read through it slowly and carefully. I had already seen a copy of his actual will that had been witnessed by Guillot and had turned up in the first batch of boxes that I had examined in Bordeaux. It was fascinating from a historical perspective but had no bearing on our search for the missing necklace. This draft was almost identical except for a paragraph that he appeared to have left out of the final document. Suppressing my excitement I read carefully about a hiding place here in the eaves of this house. It described the exact location of a stone and gave instructions how it was to be turned and twisted to reveal a hollowed out area. It spoke of a valued object within. My shouts of excitement were misunderstood and both Patrice and Guilbert raced into the room with guns already drawn. After a few grumbles from them I explained what I had found. Gaston led the way to the loft ladder that had been installed and reaching for a hooked pole pulled down the wooden staircase.

There was no light up there at all so he had brought a couple of torches that he had in a drawer. I had photographed the relevant page so I pulled out my iPhone and read through it again. Sure enough, the brick that he described could be seen in the gable wall. When I touched it, it seemed to be as firm as all of the others. If I didn't have the instructions in front of me I wouldn't have given it a second glance, but of course the likelihood was that it would be empty anyway. If anybody had seen the notes they would have looked for themselves. It really depended on how long the bible had been stored away up here. There seemed to be a gentle irony in the fact that the hiding place and the instructions for finding it had been kept only yards apart. I offered the next step to Gaston, but he refused insisting that it had been my idea that had led us here. I twisted and pulled as per instruction and sure enough the stone began to move. In front of me was a hole that was easily large enough to put my hand into. Now there is a perceived wisdom about shoving your hand into a hole that could contain anything, but I never even gave it a thought. I reached in and found nothing. I groaned in disappointment, but as I was about to pull my hand out I realised that the back of the hole dropped away into a second smaller space. I reached further and this time touched something. The object was wrapped in a cloth of some kind and when I pulled it out, it was covered in a thick layer of dust. It had not been disturbed for some time, possibly even since it had been put there. With both torches being shone down onto the package I carefully started to unwrap the cloth.

Once again I groaned in disappointment as lying in front of me was another book. This one was bound in leather but had no title on the cover. Inside were dozens of pages of handwriting. It was the journal of the last years of Antoine's life.

At this point Guilbert and Patrice decided to leave us to the 'old book' and return to Paris. Nothing had been seen by the surveillance teams so they were going to extend the search for Lillian.

It took several hours to read through the pages. It described his retirement from the law and how he had settled down to a sedentary life with just the occasional visit to see his old friend in Bordeaux. In places there were references to his earlier life that were intriguing, an escape from Versailles, a storm that blew him to Portugal and his life there. I was slowed down by Gaston who wanted to know what I had read every few pages, but I was coming to the end with no mention of a necklace when I read the following.

June 17th 1825

'At last I feel free of the weight that I have been carrying around for all of these years. Ten years of searching for the rightful owners, Bohem and Bassange, who were destroyed by the trust that they placed in the Queen and her followers. I have been unable to find them. They bought the stones out of their own pocket, created a beautiful object, handed it over and received nothing in return. They have disappeared, died, who knows? I cannot put this situation right by returning the necklace to them so if they cannot have it, no-one shall. It now rests in the mud at the bottom of the Seine. As my life comes to its end so does the life of the Queen's necklace.'

I slumped back in my chair. Gaston had been reading over my shoulder and laughed out loud.

'So Motte has been wasting his time and effort over nothing. Perhaps he will leave Lillian alone now?'

I wasn't so sure. He was a vindictive, nasty little man and my guess was that this would just trigger him into passing

Lillian's file on. Of course I didn't say so and just agreed with Gaston's hopes.

The kitchen door was not quite closed so we clearly heard the sound of a key in the outside door lock. Patrice and Guilbert were not due to return for several more hours and in any case they would have warned us first. There wasn't time to go and hide in the loft space so I grabbed a kitchen knife from the block and turned to face the door. We had been surprised by Motte once before, but it wasn't going to happen again. Gaston was fumbling with his mobile phone as he tried to contact Patrice. There were no voices so maybe it was just one person that we could hear in the corridor. The kitchen door swung open and Lillian stepped through.

She looked tired and her clothes were crumpled and she was as startled to see us as we were to see her. It didn't help that I had a large carving knife in my hand which I casually tried to return to the block. For a moment I thought that she was going to burst into tears, but instead a big grin split her face.

'I've sorted it. It's over.'

We spoke at the same time.
   'What do you mean 'You've sorted it'?'
   'What's over?'

She simply repeated herself.
   'I've sorted it. It's over.'
   Then she added, 'Everything. Pour me a glass of wine and I'll tell you what happened.'

We had to curb our impatience for several minutes while Lillian took a large gulp of Burgundy and gathered her thoughts. She started out with a question.

'Do you know what a computer worm is?'

It didn't take either of us a great deal of thought before answering, 'No'.

'OK. A worm is a type of computer program but is designed to self replicate. If there is a network connection to a machine either internally within an organisation or to the internet a worm can be designed to copy itself onto other computers. It is a more malicious variety of the malware that Motte had me writing for him. When a worm spreads it isn't a problem, it's what the worm does on each machine that it infects that is interesting. In theory it's possible to create a worm that can do anything from copying files to deleting an entire operating system and rendering the computer dead. They are used by criminals and the military for a variety of effects. For example it's widely thought that a worm known as Stuxnet was used by the Americans to substantially slow down Iran's nuclear program. They are complicated to write but it occurred to me that if I could create one with the correct characteristics I could use it to solve my problem. The difficulty with the file that Motte had created was that he would have back up copies spread throughout his online accounts and without knowing the location of every last one I couldn't hope to delete them all. My worm, which I called 'Gaston', was designed to spread each time a file containing my name was uploaded from his computer. It then deletes those files and any that had been uploaded previously.'

Our reaction was interesting. Gaston didn't know whether to be flattered or insulted having a worm named after him, albeit simply thousands of lines of computer code rather than a wriggly garden thing. My concern was the gaping hole that I could see.

'What's to stop him simply recreating it? I know that some of the evidence was real but some was also fabricated. If he's malicious enough he could simply repeat what he had done and you would be no better off.'

This time a sip rather than a gulp of the rich red wine.

'Ah yes. I had been working on that premise too and although I believed that he was dead when I left Lisbon, I had already built into 'Gaston' some code that would make public some files that he had, files that referred to his Rosicrucian friends. As you know, he has powerful allies who don't tolerate fools gladly. I guessed that he is the sort of person who would have kept information on them as well. That was what held me up. I needed to get into his computer at his house to check what was there and then install my program. My hope was that the threat of this material being sent out to newspapers and conspiracy websites would stop him recreating my file. It worked, but not as I expected. My plan was to break in and access his computer via his internet router. It's an old trick, but one that usually works. Instead I was caught by one of his staff who rang him in Portugal. I had seen him killed just a few days earlier or so I thought, so I was floored when he answered. Fortunately he told them to detain me until he returned. They put me back into the guest accommodation again, but didn't take my rucksack. If they had I would have had to break in to his office instead. The first time that I was there I had seen an extender for the internet router in the corridor. I waited for the early hours of the morning and tried to be subtle at first, but picking locks isn't as easy as they make out. In the end I just put my boot against the door and persuaded it that it wanted to open. Cabling in my laptop gave me access to anything that was connected to the router including his own machine. I looked through his files and there was a ton of incriminating material. I then injected the worm and left him a message telling him what I had done. It's a lot easier breaking out of a place than it is breaking in I can tell you. I called in on a friend of mine and made sure that he would release everything if anything happened to me before I had a chance to automate it. I left there this morning and came back here. OK - so now you are up to date. What about you two? I bet nothing very interesting has happened here.'

Gaston and I looked at each other and burst out laughing. It was our turn to drink wine and tell a story.

It was two days later, back in Locquirec, that I had the first of several ideas. Patrice and Guilbert had dropped us off here in Brittany then headed back to Montignac. They had indicated that if I were moving to Brittany they would prefer to stay there and if I were agreeable they were happy to stay on as caretakers for the chateau. It was rarely that I seriously needed them, but when I did I really needed them. In between those occasions the chateau needed to be looked after so it suited me perfectly. It was William's legacy to me and I had no intention of selling it, even if I wasn't living there. I still didn't know whether Beckford was telling the truth about William being a member of their order, but even if this were true I didn't believe that he was of their like. My memories were of a kind, caring and gentle man.

Gaston and Lillian had stayed for a few days longer and it was while we were sat talking in the garden I put forward a suggestion.

* * *

'As it stands you have a friend who will release Motte's files should anything happen to you. Why don't we put a second layer in place. I have a very good friend who is a lawyer in Paris. We could leave an envelope with her with instructions, 'Only To Be Opened in the case of ......'

So far so good. My next proposal left Gaston at a loss for words.

'Since we seem to drink so much wine, I have decided to buy a small vineyard in Bordeaux. What's more I know just the person to run it for us. I think it's time Gaston for you to come with me and meet Sophie Guillot.'

It was Lillian however, who had the last word.

'I spent most of yesterday 'facetiming' with Shirley and her boyfriend Andres. I hadn't realised that he was a lecturer in Computer Science. He told me that there are scholarships available for overseas students to study computing at his university and he's prepared to put me forward for a place.'

We couldn't match that. She did have the last word.

Disclaimer

If you enjoyed Converging Lines, the first book in the series 'Mirrors' is also available from Amazon.

This is a work of fiction. All of the characters, organisations, and events portrayed in this novel are either products of the author's imagination or are used fictitiously.

CONVERGING LINES

.

Printed in Great Britain
by Amazon